THE DRAG
THE PEARL

Barbara Cartland

Barbara Cartland Ebooks Ltd

This edition © 2023

ISBNs

9781788676700   EPUB

9781788676717   PAPERBACK

Book design by M-Y Books
m-ybooks.co.uk

THE BARBARA CARTLAND ETERNAL COLLECTION

The Barbara Cartland Eternal Collection is the unique opportunity to collect all five hundred of the timeless beautiful romantic novels written by the world's most celebrated and enduring romantic author.

Named the Eternal Collection because Barbara's inspiring stories of pure love, just the same as love itself, the books will be published on the internet at the rate of four titles per month until all five hundred are available.

The Eternal Collection, classic pure romance available worldwide for all time .

THE LATE DAME BARBARA CARTLAND

Barbara Cartland, who sadly died in May 2000 at the grand age of ninety eight, remains one of the world's most famous romantic novelists. With worldwide sales of over one billion, her outstanding 723 books have been translated into thirty six different languages, to be enjoyed by readers of romance globally.

Writing her first book 'Jigsaw' at the age of 21, Barbara became an immediate bestseller. Building upon this initial success, she wrote continuously throughout her life, producing bestsellers for an astonishing 76 years. In addition to Barbara Cartland's legion of fans in the UK and across Europe, her books have always been immensely popular in the USA. In 1976 she achieved the unprecedented feat of having books at numbers 1 & 2 in the prestigious B. Dalton Bookseller bestsellers list.

Although she is often referred to as the 'Queen of Romance', Barbara Cartland also wrote several historical biographies, six autobiographies and numerous theatrical plays as well as books on life, love, health and cookery. Becoming one of Britain's most popular media personalities and dressed in her trademark pink, Barbara spoke on radio and television about social and political issues, as well as making many public appearances.

In 1991 she became a Dame of the Order of the British Empire for her contribution to literature and her work for humanitarian and charitable causes.

Known for her glamour, style, and vitality Barbara Cartland became a legend in her own lifetime. Best remembered for her wonderful romantic novels and loved by millions of readers worldwide, her books remain treasured for their heroic heroes, plucky heroines and traditional values. But above all, it was Barbara Cartland's overriding belief in the positive power of love to help, heal and improve the quality of life for everyone that made her truly unique.

AUTHOR'S NOTE

All the events and the majority of the characters in this novel are factual.

The Allied troops entered Peking on the night of April the thirteenth 1901 and the British Legation after a fifty-five day siege was relieved the following day.

Those imprisoned in the Legation were able to survive owing to the foresight of Herbert Squiers, the First Secretary at the American Legation who had bought large quantities of food before the siege began.

At daybreak the Dowager Empress, dressed as a peasant, left the Forbidden City in a cart with the Emperor and the ferrety Prince Tuan in another. And only a handful of eunuchs went with them.

Peking was looted by the troops and Chinese soldiers. What they could not carry away they burnt. The Powers behaved with magnanimity and agreed diplomatically with Li Hung-Chang that what had happened was a Boxer Rebellion against the authority of the Throne.

On this basis the Dowager Empress's part in the events could be overlooked. Somewhat grudgingly she agreed and handed over Prince Tuan, together with some other Boxer leaders for punishment. He was exiled.

Reparation had to be made in the sum of sixty-seven million pounds for two hundred dead Missionaries and thirty thousand Chinese converts.

After Li Hung-Chang had sealed the last of the agreements with the foreign Powers, he then collapsed and died.

The Dowager Empress ordered that a Shrine should be built in Peking in his honour.

On November fourteenth, 1908, the weak and ineffectual Emperor passed into the Hall of his Ancestors and the next day, as the astrologers had prophesied, the Dowager Empress followed him.

CHAPTER ONE
1900

"I cannot think why you are so apprehensive, Major Ware," Sir Claude Macdonald said.

"The Prime Minister has heard many rumours that there is a great deal of unrest in the Provinces."

"There is always unrest in China and I can readily assure you that, as British Minister, I am perfectly able to cope with any situation that may arise from it."

Sir Claude Macdonald spoke almost sharply as if he fancied that his authority was being questioned.

Stanton Ware, looking at him, thought that the Prime Minister was surely correct to have insinuated that he was not the right man in the right place.

The Marquis of Salisbury had been too tactful to say very much, but then his advisors in the Foreign Office had been blunt and the Press more so.

The Correspondent of *The Times* had written,

"*Everyone denounced the appointment. Sir Claude was attacked as imperfectly educated, weak, flippant and garrulous, the type of Military Officer rolled out a mile at a time and then lopped off in six-foot lengths!*"

Stanton Ware had laughed when he read it, but now he looked at Sir Claude Macdonald speculatively, feeling that he would be quite unable to cope if things got out of hand, as was to be expected in China.

It was in point of fact a tragedy that at this moment the British should be represented by a Minister who had no previous experience of China except as a gunnery instructor in Hong Kong.

Sir Claude was, as one of his critics had described him, 'a stringy, bleary-eyed beanpole with a exaggeratedly waxed moustache.'

There was no doubt about the moustache and Sir Claude twirled it conceitedly as he said,

"You can most certainly inform the Prime Minister, Major Ware, that everything is under control and that the few incidents that have occurred are really of little consequence."

Stanton Ware paused before he replied,

"I think that the murder of Brooks might be considered important, particularly to him."

"Brooks was a Missionary," Sir Claude answered, "and the Missionaries have indeed been a cause of trouble in China ever since they were allowed into the country in 1860. The Chinese resent it that they undermine their traditional ancestor-worship, which to them is of the deepest importance."

"I am well aware of that," Stanton Ware replied, "but then unfortunately the Chinese Christians ignore local feelings in a number of different ways."

He was thinking how the Missionaries had requisitioned Chinese Temples by declaring that they were formerly Church property and, having been given permission to build, chose conspicuous and hallowed sites on purpose.

The Franciscans even tried to collect arrears of rent for the last three hundred years!

"Again may I say that I think such things are of very little significance," Sir Claude said. "What really concerns

~2~

us is the Balance of Power, which was upset four years ago when the Russian warships sailed into Port Arthur on the coast of China."

This, Stanton Ware knew, was certainly true.

The five great Powers were jostling for position in China and were, in the words of one of the caricaturists, 'carving her up like a melon'.

It was only jealousy amongst the Westerners themselves and their incessant rivalry that prevented more of China being annexed than had been already.

Yet Stanton Ware indeed knew that in Peking, the great Northern Capital of the Celestial Empire, the Manchus fooled themselves into believing that they were strong and that Chinese ways could overcome foreign ways.

In fact, as one man in the Foreign Office had said,

"The Manchus are arrogant and weak, the Europeans are arrogant and strong. The result will be war!"

As if he knew that Stanton Ware was not convinced that there was no crisis, Sir Claude said,

"I am certain that we can trust the Dowager Empress to deal successfully with internal difficulties."

"Trust the Dowager Empress?" Stanton Ware repeated in astonishment. "You cannot be serious! The reports arriving in London make it quite clear that the Empress is, although she does not admit it, violently anti-foreign."

Sir Claude laughed and again twirled his moustache.

"My dear Major, the Dowager Empress invited my wife and other ladies of the Legation to tea in the Forbidden City to celebrate her birthday and to cement good relations between East and West."

He smiled, assuming that Stanton Ware was unaware of this and then went on,

"The Empress, or 'the Old Buddha', for that is how we usually refer to her, presented each of her guests with a huge pearl ring set in gold and offered them a jade cup of tea with both hands."

"Very generous," Stanton Ware muttered ironically.

"It was a symbolic gesture," Sir Claude explained. "The Empress drank from it first, then passed it on, murmuring, 'one family, all one family'."

"And you believe her?"

Sir Claude shrugged his shoulders.

"I can see no reason to do otherwise."

"Despite the fact that the Boxers are growing in size every day?'

Sir Claude laughed.

"The Society of the Righteous and Harmonious Fists, who we call for short 'the Boxers', is made up of youths none that much older than nineteen. They are centred in the Northern Provinces, particularly on the borders of Shantung and Chilihi."

"They are, I hear, on the move."

"To where?" Sir Claude asked with a gesture of his large hand. "Because they pretend to have magic powers, the ignorant Chinese follow them, but to anyone of intelligence they can be little but a joke."

"I think it is a joke that we shall not find at all funny," Stanton Ware said sternly. "To get down to brass tacks, do you, Minister, require extra troops to be sent out here to protect, if nothing else, the British Legation?"

Sir Claude laughed.

"Extra troops? The ones we have have little enough to do. All I can say, Major Ware, is that you are making mountains out of molehills or seeing real Dragons when they are nothing but paper ones."

He laughed heartily at his own joke.

Stanton Ware then rose to his feet.

"Thank you for giving me so much of your time, Minister. I shall report what you have said to the Prime Minister. I am very sure he will be interested."

"You are returning home?" Sir Claude asked.

"Not immediately," he replied vaguely. "I have some friends who I wish to see and then I might go to Tientsin and take a ship from there to Hong Kong."

"Then *bon voyage*," Sir Claude said. "It is very nice to have met you, Major Ware. I hope you enjoy your visit to Peking."

Stanton Ware bowed and left the Legation.

He had expected to find the British Minister obtuse, obstinate and pig-headed, but he had not imagined him to be quite such a fool as he had proved himself to be in their conversation.

That same evening a telegram in strict code was sent to the Foreign Office requesting the urgent despatch of 'new parts for the machine'.

Stanton Ware went back to where he was staying and sat down for a short while to think over what he had just heard together with what he already knew about the situation in China before he had arrived.

He was very experienced in the affairs of the East and so when the Prime Minister, the Marquis of Salisbury, had become perturbed at what he had learnt from other sources, it was inevitable that someone would say,

"Send for Major Stanton Ware!"

It had not been convenient for Stanton Ware and he had obeyed the summons somewhat grudgingly.

But when the Prime Minister had spoken frankly and Stanton Ware saw the reports from British Agents all over China, he then realised that this was exactly the sort of assignment that really interested him.

Also he saw that he could not have been paid a bigger compliment than being asked to undertake it.

At thirty-three he had made himself an expert on the affairs of the Far East and spoke fluently almost every major language and dialect that might be required of him.

He had made many expeditions into unknown and dangerous places and had emerged successful and alive from so many situations that would have undoubtedly defeated or killed another man that his luck had already become a legend amongst his contemporaries.

"We are all extremely grateful to you, Major Ware, for all that you have achieved in Afghanistan," the Prime Minister had said on parting. "I will perhaps be forgiven for letting you into the secret when I tell you that your name has been put forward in the New Year's Honours List for a K.C.M.G. from Queen Victoria."

He could not tell by the expression on Stanton Ware's face whether he was pleased or not by the information that he was to be a Knight Commander of St. Michael and St. George, an ancient Order of Chivalry.

He merely bowed, murmured some words of thanks, then left before the Prime Minister could say anything more.

'Strange chap!' the Marquis of Salisbury had said to himself when he was alone. 'But undoubtedly an extremely efficient one.'

It was typical of Stanton Ware that, faced with a problem of which only he realised the magnitude, he should sit relaxed so that he could think before he took any form of action.

Only a few people were aware that he had spent two years of his life studying Yoga and being taught the secrets of Oriental Meditation by a Lama in one of the great Lamaseries in the East.

It was this training which not only kept him physically in the peak of condition, but also gave him an acute perception and a mind which the Chinese described as 'seeing the world behind the world'.

Stanton Ware did not pretend to magic or even clairvoyant powers, but he undoubtedly used what the Tibetans called 'The Third Eye'.

It was a sense which all human beings used to have until they lost it by grasping after materialistic things and putting the physical before the spiritual.

Like a man considering one of the Chinese puzzles carved in ivory that might take a lifetime to solve, Stanton Ware sat now thinking over what he knew and what he sensed. He found it far more disturbing than he had even imagined because the Officials on the spot, like the British Minister, were blind to the potential dangers ahead.

*

In the growing darkness a sedan chair was being carried through the streets of the City. Peking rose amongst groves of white pines on a level plain less than one hundred miles South of the Great Wall where it runs from West to East in Northern China.

It was built against grassy banks of hills that climbed in waves to the North and to the West and in the fertile and misty hollows nestled Temples and Palaces.

When travellers first entered Peking through the South gate of the outer or Chinese City, they found it very different from the beauty of the exterior.

All along the broad street that led to the Imperial City there were mat-shed booths and shops huddled three rows deep. Flags announcing their wares streamed out in the breeze and beggars in organised gangs accosted passers-by.

Looking from behind the curtains that veiled the window of his chair, Stanton Ware saw the rope-dancers twirling and spinning as the pickpockets worked among the gaping crowds.

There were clairvoyants selling almanacs of lucky days and the peddlers carrying yoked panniers of sweets, needles, toys, tea, rice cakes and fans.

There were craftsmen mending porcelain with rivets, chiropodists and barbers, scribes, quacks and, inevitably as the Chinese crowd so loved them, acrobats and jugglers sometimes accompanied by bears and monkeys.

To Stanton Ware it was all very familiar and had an attraction all of its own.

He had almost forgotten, he thought, the smell of roasting meat and game, of ginseng, soy, garlic and tobacco, which seemed to hang over the streets in clouds.

The sedan chair wove in and out of all the traffic of Peking carts, wheelbarrows, donkeys struggling under mountainous loads and camels from Mongolia.

It was China as the majority of Chinese saw it, complete with barefoot ragged beggars and the watchmen with their lanterns and clappers.

Soon Stanton Ware was carried away from the crowded roadway into a part of the City where the houses looked much more prosperous and finally the chair was set down outside the '*House of a Thousand Joys*'.

As always in China there was no ostentatious indication of what the house contained.

In fact the exterior was dull and almost dingy and only when Stanton Ware stepped out of the sedan chair, paid its attendant well and the door opened for him did he find the interior very different.

Within the outer door there was another of scarlet, decorated with rows of knobs in fives.

Inside there was, Stanton Ware knew, a regular Chinese house consisting of nine or ten courtyards spread over a large area each with three or four one-storey pavilions around them.

The '*House of a Thousand Joys*' was unique in that each small pavilion with its exquisite white latticework, its tiny courtyard with a gold-fish pool, was allotted to a beautiful woman.

The servant who admitted him stared curiously at Stanton Ware for he was enveloped in a long cloak, which covered not only his body but had also a hood that concealed most of his face.

"I would see Diverse Delight," he began.

"Honoured sir, if you will come this way I will see if Diverse Delight is free to receive you."

The servant led Stanton Ware into a room exquisitely furnished in the Chinese manner with low tables, cushions on the floor and paintings on the walls that he knew were of great antiquity and value.

There was one that he had always liked particularly of mountains in the mist painted in ink on silk by Hung Hsien in the seventeenth century.

He knew that every stroke had a special inner meaning and would not only be esoteric to the painter but would evoke a response that was different in each person who beheld it

He had been taught long ago that in a picture small objects like a bird, a flower or a fish were all painted to stress their growing and moving life and their involvement with all living things.

He was puzzling out for himself what Hung Hsien's picture meant to him now when the servant returned.

"Diverse Delight will see you, Honoured Sir," he said, bowing.

He led Stanton Ware through complicated passages, past pavilions where lovely women with intriguing names sat surrounded by beauty.

There was one he remembered, called 'Happy Hours', another 'Celestial Flower' and a third 'Sweet Submission'.

He was led almost through the whole length of the house before he was shown into a room furnished with rare specimens of the craftsman's art in wood and priceless lacquer.

The hangings were of rich silk embroidered with many flying phoenixes and Dragons and against them there were porcelain urns in which dwarf trees were growing.

But Stanton Ware had eyes only for the woman who was waiting for him and, as she entered, he could see a look of enquiry on her face, which was instantly replaced by the light of recognition.

She bowed very low, then there was a smile on her red lips as she said,

"I had hoped, but I could not be sure even from the servant's description, that it was you, Noble One, whom I have missed for so many moons."

Stanton Ware threw back the hood of his cloak and unclasped it at the neck.

The servant took it from him, moving so quietly that it seemed as if he was attended by invisible hands.

Then he was sitting down on one of the low cushioned seats with a glass of Samshu wine in front of him.

"You have been away a long time?" Diverse Delight asked.

It was not an accusation but a regret.

"I have come back because I understand there is trouble."

"I guessed that was why you came to see me."

"I should have come anyway," he said truthfully, "but you know that I need your help."

"What do you wish to know?"

"Need you ask? What is happening in China? What are all these rumours that grow more ominous month by month?"

"You are right. They are indeed ominous and I might have guessed that sooner or later you would come and see what you could do about them."

"And what can I do?"

Diverse Delight made a gesture that was explicit without words.

Then she said in a low voice,

"We all know that the year 1900 has been marked for misfortune."

"That is what I want you to tell me about."

"There are evil astrological omens," she said, "and those who look in the crystal ball speak not only of blood but of disaster for China."

"What sort of disaster?" Stanton Ware asked her.

He seemed relaxed and he sipped his Samshu with pleasure because the wine was to his liking.

At the same time his mind was alert, aware that Diverse Delight could tell him much that he wished to know and no one was in a better position to do so.

The '*House of a Thousand Joys*' was the most exclusive, most expensive and important 'House of Flowers' in the whole of China.

There had been whispers that the Emperor himself, before he was made a prisoner by his aunt in the Ying T'ai or 'Ocean Palace', had very often in disguise visited the '*House of a Thousand Joys.*'

It was certainly patronised by all the most important Court Officials and Mandarins of Peking besides those who came to the Capital from the country.

They had heard stories of the joys that they would find if they sampled the hospitality of Diverse Delight.

When a man had drunk a lot he could be tempted to discuss affairs of State with girls who were trained to be sympathetic and understanding in a way that few other women could be.

Stanton Ware had often been asked by those who were curious about Chinese customs why any Mandarin or Court Official should bother to be interested in women such as could be found in the '*House of a Thousand Joys*'.

"After all they do have any number of concubines at their disposal," was an inevitable remark.

But the concubines either in the Forbidden City or those who belonged to rich Mandarins and merchants had no contact with the outside world.

Their whole life and their whole interest, was centred round their Master and, apart from the beauty of their bodies, they could be extremely dull.

But the girls in the '*House of a Thousand Joys*' were chosen not only for their attractions but also for their intelligence.

As a result Diverse Delight was without exception one of the best-informed women in the whole of Northern China.

"Tell me the position if you will," Stanton Ware requested now.

There was a note in his voice and a smile on his lips that many women all over the world had found irresistible.

"You are incorrigible, Noble One," Diverse Delight said with a laugh. "You come and go as you please, you leave me wondering whether you are alive or dead, then you return and squeeze me dry like a pomegranate!"

Stanton Ware took her hand and raised it to his lips.

"You have never failed me in all the years we have known each other," he said, "and I cannot believe you will do so now."

She gave a little sigh.

"I suppose it would be impossible to say 'no', even if I wished to do so. What do you wish to hear?"

"Everything," he answered. "As you know I have been away from China for over two years now and things have changed."

"They have indeed – and for the worse."

"That is what I heard before I left England."

"You know that all progress in China has been suspended? The Dowager Empress has informed the Powers that no more railroads are to be built and it would therefore be useless for foreign representatives to submit any such proposals."

"I heard that too," Stanton Ware murmured.

"No railroads – no progress."

"Naturally!"

"There was only one way in which Her Majesty was prepared to deal with the West – by the arms of war!"

Again Stanton Ware nodded.

"She has told the Generals to adopt Western techniques and buy Western armaments. Do you know why?" Diverse Delight asked.

"You tell me," he answered, "I am here to listen."

"To rid China of foreigners!"

"I doubt if China has the strength to do so," Stanton Ware said slowly.

"But you have not enough arms or enough troops here now," Diverse Delight replied, "to stem the flood tide when it engulfs you."

It is what Stanton Ware had thought himself, but he was surprised that Diverse Delight should be aware of it.

"The Dowager Empress throws up dust into the eyes of the foreigner," she went on in a low voice, "but the Boxers are rousing the crowds to follow them and everywhere they go they shout, 'burn, *burn*! Kill, *kill*!'"

"How strong are they?" Stanton Ware enquired.

"Men fight very well when they have faith," Diverse Delight answered, "and their magic convinces those who are stupid enough to be deceived by blank cartridges and arrows which pierce but do not hurt people in a trance."

Stanton Ware did not speak and she added,

"They also spread rumours, which the Chinese are always ready to believe."

"What sort of rumours?"

"That the iron roads and the iron carriages of the railways are disturbing the terrestrial Dragon and destroying the earth's beneficial influences."

Stanton Ware smiled, knowing that primitive peoples are always afraid of trains the first time they see them.

"They say that the red liquid dripping from the 'iron snake', which is the rust water from the oxidated telegraph wire, is the blood of the spirits of the outraged air."

"Can anyone really believe such nonsense?" Stanton Ware asked.

"They teach that the Missionaries extract the eyes, the marrow and the hearts of the dead in order to make medicaments and whoever drinks a glass of tea at a Parsonage is stricken by death, his brain bursts out of his skull!"

She looked away from him as she continued in a low voice,

"The Boxers also say that the children received into the orphanages are killed and their intestines are used to change lead into silver and make precious remedies."

"The people who believe such things must be very stupid," Stanton Ware commented.

At the same time he had not forgotten the trouble the Missionaries had caused in the past.

"You say that the Boxers are gaining strength," he said after a short pause. "Surely the Empress does not support such riff-raff?"

"Officially she says they must be constrained and not allowed to increase."

"But unofficially?" Stanton Ware questioned.

"When some Officials treated the Boxers as rebels and attempted to disperse them, the Governor of the Province flew into a rage and claimed they were the patriotic Militia that 'the Old Buddha' had asked for a month or so ago."

"Who can make the Empress see the danger in such a policy?" Stanton Ware asked her.

Diverse Delight made a helpless gesture with her small soft hands before she replied,

"That is not for me to say, but something will have to be done and done quickly if the prophecies of disaster to China are to be disproved."

She spoke earnestly and Stanton Ware knew that she genuinely loved her country apart from the fact that riots and fighting in Peking itself would be extremely bad for business.

"Is there no Official brave enough to be frank with the Empress and show her that she must make a stand against these young hooligans before it is too late?"

"The Emperor wanted to make changes, but he lost his struggle to promote progress and those who followed him were put to death or exiled, and the rest have become afraid."

"All of them?" Stanton Ware asked.

"There is Li Hung-Chang!"

Stanton Ware nodded.

He knew that Li Hung-Chang had been among the Emperor's trusted Officials and was China's most progressive leader.

He had encouraged the building of arsenals, dockyards and warships and five years ago in 1895 he had gone to Japan to negotiate the Treaty that ended the Sino-Japanese War.

He admired what he saw in Japan for that country had been modernising her ways for many years.

Stanton Ware had been told by Japan's Prince Ito how Li Hung-Chang had summed up the problems of China.

"My country is hampered by traditions and customs," he had said, "and now there are too many Provinces with strong sectionalism."

He had been too loyal to mention the terrible power struggle within the Imperial family.

But even after the Emperor was rendered powerless, Li Hung-Chang had gone on trying to bring forward new ideas and trying to persuade the obstinate Dowager not to keep China still living in the Dark Ages.

He was too important to China for the Empress to dispense with him altogether.

But she appointed him Viceroy of Kwang Tung and Kwangi in the South of the country, which was as good a way as any of keeping him out of the Council Chambers in Peking.

Nevertheless, at seventy-seven years of age, he was still a power in the land and still held the respect of a great number of thinking Chinese.

"How can I see him?" Stanton Ware now asked.

Diverse Delight made a little gesture that was more expressive than the shrug beloved of the French people and had a grace that was peculiarly Chinese.

Then she exclaimed,

"Wait, I have an idea! A very close friend of Li Hung-Chang is Tseng-Wen, a Mandarin living here in Peking who is a man of great power in many spheres. When Li Hung-Chang comes to visit the Dowager Empress, he always calls on his friend."

"I would very much like to meet him," Stanton Ware proposed.

"You shall do so for he is a friend of mine and what could be happier than that I should be the link between two such dear people – you and he?"

"And how shall I thank you?" Stanton Ware asked in his deep voice.

"What can I ask?" she replied.

He thought that, like a flower that comes into bloom, she was even more attractive now than when he had known her first when she was a very young girl.

He threw out his hands eloquently and gave the traditional Eastern reply,

"All that I have is yours!"

She took one of his hands in both of hers, turned it upwards and, bending her dark head, touched his palm with her forehead.

*

The house of Tseng-Wen was very impressive and it was quite obvious from the moment that the sedan chair set him down outside that it belonged to a man of wealth and importance.

Stanton Ware was attired in a brocade coat that was worn by most Manchus during the winter months.

On his head he had the black turned-up hat affected by Generals and Statesmen.

He was in disguise not on his own account, but merely because he thought that it would be embarrassing for Tseng-Wen to be seen receiving a foreigner.

Although the Boxer influence had not yet reached Peking, the anti-foreigner atmosphere was very evident, as Stanton Ware had found everywhere he went.

If he walked in the streets, he could hear mutters from the people he passed by and in the shops the salesmen, not knowing that he spoke Chinese, would often say while he waited for attention,

"Who's to attend to the foreign devil?"

There were murmurs and whispers and many stealthy movements that had certainly not been evident when he had last visited Peking.

Although they were small things in themselves, he knew that all together they constituted an ever-growing threat for peaceful relations that were essential if the five Western Powers were to continue trading in China.

Trade was of vital importance to the Chinese themselves even if the Dowager Empress might be too stupid to realise it.

It was in fact the weakness of the Manchu Dynasty that had allowed the foreigners to take over great chunks of Chinese territory.

It was not entirely unreasonable that there should be a deep suspicion that foreign ways would bring disaster to the Chinese Empire.

But it seemed almost impossible to explain to the ruling group that the best future for China lay in following the West in the development of its railroads and telegraph and in the possession of modern ships and arms.

As Stanton Ware had lived among the ordinary people in the East, he could understand their looking to magic to alleviate their fears and relieve their poverty.

The corruption and the wild extravagances of those in power were bleeding the country of its greatest assets.

It was also causing a hidden resentment in those who suffered from the exorbitant taxes that, if it burst into flames, it could bring destruction and disaster in its train.

Stanton Ware had not discussed with the British Minister a placard that had been posted in the town of Hien in the Province of Chihli the previous year.

It had said,

"*The patriots of all Provinces, seeing the men of the West transgress all limits in their behaviour, have decided to assemble on the fifteenth day of the fourth moon and to kill the Westerners and burn down their houses. Those whose hearts are not in accord with us are scoundrels and of bad character.*"

It had aroused little interest either in Peking or in London when this was reported by the Jesuit Missionaries.

But Stanton Ware had realised that it was the beginning and he knew now that, because no action had been taken, the Boxers had begun to gather strength.

He hoped however that even at this late hour something could be done to save China.

But he had known as soon as he arrived that the sands were running out.

He thought without conceit that he should have been sent for very much earlier.

On his way to the house of Tseng-Wen he had been turning over in his mind all he knew about Li Hung-Chang and felt that if anyone could help it would be the aged Viceroy.

He entered Tseng-Wen's house and realised at once that he was expected.

There was a courtyard planted with dwarf trees and he was taken to a room that was very large and lofty.

The floor was covered with thick magnificent carpets as it was winter, but they would be replaced in summer with floor coverings of delicately painted woven bamboo peelings, which were both cool and clear.

There were scrolls and paintings on the walls that Stanton Ware longed to examine and a fine collection of exquisite jade which he knew was beyond price.

Then the door opened and an old Chinese gentleman with a grey beard entered.

The moment he looked at him, Stanton Ware, who was used to judging a person on sight, realised here was a man he would both trust and like.

Because in the East it is bad manners to be hurried, they exchanged many bows.

Then the Mandarin dusted with the rich silk of his robe the spotless seat of the chair that Stanton Ware was to occupy and Stanton Ware did the same for his host.

Then they both bowed again and finally took their places.

A servant brought wine and the delicious little sweetmeats which were customary.

They were set in front of them on a low table and the porcelain plates they were served on were so exquisite that Stanton Ware could hardly forbear to comment on them.

He knew, however, that that would be considered discourteous and then he waited for Tseng-Wen to speak.

His old face was sad and careworn and there were deep lines under his eyes.

"My son, you have come at a sad time," he said slowly. "My heart is heavy for the future of our country. There is a dark hour at hand and yet my friend from the '*House of a Thousand Joys*' tells me that if anyone can avert the holocaust it would be you."

"You honour me, Noble Sir," Stanton Ware replied. "I have come to seek your wisdom."

Tseng-Wen sighed.

"What we say to each other must not be known outside this room."

He lowered his voice before he went on,

"Her Majesty the Dowager Empress is of the belief that the hope of deliverance for our country lies in the Boxers. Since I ventured to disagree with her, a cloud has passed before the sun and I live in darkness."

"Her Majesty really believes that?" Stanton Ware asked him.

The old man nodded.

"She has always been very superstitious," he said. "She consults many Oracles and many clairvoyants."

"But surely she knows that this has been prophesied as a year of disaster?" Stanton Ware interposed.

Tseng-Wen sighed again.

"The Empress, you understand, has many unscrupulous people around her and they tell her what she wishes to hear."

Stanton Ware was quite certain that this was true and there would be many Officials in the Forbidden City who would find it to their own advantage to keep the Dowager Empress ignorant of many things that were happening in the country outside.

"But surely," he said, "the Empress really cannot believe in the ridiculous image of the Boxers?"

Tseng-Wen shook his head in anguish.

"I am told by one who knows," he replied, "that she repeats the Boxer charm seventy times a day."

"What is that?" Stanton Ware asked.

The old Mandarin hesitated as if he could not soil his lips with the words, then he recited in a low voice,

"*I am the Spirit of the cold cloud, behind me lies the Deity of fire. Invoke the black Gods of pestilence.*"

He looked at Stanton Ware with darkness in his eyes as he added,

"Every time Her Majesty repeats it, her Chief Attendant shouts,

"There goes one more foreign devil!"

"It is very childish," Stanton Ware exclaimed.

"Whoever lights the fire, the pain of its burning is the same," the old man observed.

"Is there anything I can do?"

"I have been thinking of that before you came," Tseng-Wen replied. "As I expect you know already, there is only one man who, if he wished, could save China."

Stanton Ware waited, but he already knew the answer.

"Li Hung-Chang is a man I have trusted all my life," Tseng-Wen said, "although I know there are many things said about him that have spoilt his image and made those in the West suspicious that he is not all he appears to be."

Tseng-Wen did not have to repeat the many things that Stanton Ware knew already.

It was said that Li Hung-Ghang had taken bribes, there was no denying that he was one of the richest men in China that, despite his progressive outlook, he had not supported the Emperor in his struggle against his aunt

But he had dedicated his life to the service of China and he had been almost unique in saying of the foreigners,

"They are activated by upright and amicable principles and then entertain no feelings of animosity towards China."

He was not a Manchu, like the majority of those in attendance on the Dowager Empress, in fact practically everyone involved in governing China.

He was a Han Chinese, tall commanding and a man of exceptional ambition, who spoke in the broad brogue of his native Anhwei.

Li Hung-Chang's family had been killed by the Taiping rebels and at the young age of thirty-nine he had become Governor of Kiangsu.

All his life he had fought, sometimes all alone, for the development of China as a great Power in a rapidly developing world and Stanton Ware was certain that Tseng-Wen was right when he said that the only hope now lay with Li Hung-Chang.

"How can I see him?" he asked aloud.

"It would be difficult, but it could be arranged."

"How?"

"You must not approach him as a foreigner, that would be dangerous both to you and to him. Feeling is running so high that not only might you lose your life, but Li Hung-Chang his Power."

"I have passed as a Manchu before now," Stanton Ware remarked with a smile.

"That should not be difficult for you," Tseng-Wen replied, "because Manchus, unlike the Chinese, are tall and, if you come from the Manchurian border, you will not be expected to be anything but a strong and vigorous man."

Stanton Ware waited.

"With the changing of the moon Li Hung-Chang will arrive to stay with Prince Tuan, whose Palace is at the foot of the Western Mountains, two days' journey from here."

Stanton Ware looked relieved.

He had thought that he might have to travel to the Province of Kwang Tung of which Li Hung-Chang was the Viceroy.

He was well aware that it would not only be a tedious journey but would also take so much time that he was certain that the events they feared would .take place long before he got there.

"It would be easy to visit The Palace with your generous help," Stanton Ware said. "I am very grateful."

"It is we who love China who should be thanking you. But before you leave there is much work that you and I must do together."

Stanton Ware looked surprised.

"You will not only travel disguised as a Mandarin, but Li Hung-Chang must believe you to be one."

Tseng-Wen's voice was very serious as he went on,

"If he refused to hear you and learnt you were a foreigner, your life would undoubtedly be in danger. Also I do *not* trust Prince Tuan."

Stanton Ware waited for him to continue,

"To take unnecessary risks would be the action of a fool," he said. "I have a close friend who a year ago renounced the world and retired into a Lamasery. He is a Mandarin."

Tseng-Wen took a sip of wine before he continued,

"He would I know be very proud to lend you his name and position to help our beloved country."

"I am deeply honoured," Stanton Ware murmured.

"Li Hung-Chang," the old man went on, "will wait to find out how he will be received by the Dowager Empress if he comes to the Forbidden City. As you certainly know, she is very unpredictable."

"Then I could call on him as soon as he arrives at The Palace," Stanton Ware suggested.

Tseng-Wen nodded.

"You will go to him as my friend, carrying messages and gifts from me. To be exposed would involve not only you but my friend and myself. Therefore to act the part of a Mandarin you must be a Mandarin in thought, in word and in deed."

"Honoured Sir, your wisdom is what I might have expected."

"Because it is important that you should hear not only what Li Hung-Chang has to say, but to learn other secrets which may be hidden in The Palace, I will send someone with you."

"I am overwhelmingly grateful, there is no need for me to tell you," Stanton Ware said.

"No need at all, my son," Tseng-Wen replied. "And now I would wish you to meet your companion on this extremely important journey on which the whole fate of China may hang."

As he spoke, he clapped his hands together and a servant came to the door.

The old man spoke two words.

The servant bowed and withdrew and Stanton Ware reflectively picked up his glass of wine.

He was wondering what sort of man Tseng-Wen would send with him.

It would be someone, he thought carefully, who was used to spying out the secrets of rival establishments.

Every Mandarin or man of wealth had a number of such men in his service. They spoke a complexity of languages and would usually worm themselves into the confidence of servants and minor Officials.

The door opened.

Stanton Ware deliberately set down his glass before he looked round.

He knew that from the Chinese point of view it was always a mistake to look too eager.

Then, as he slowly turned his head around, he almost betrayed himself by uttering an exclamation.

For it was not a man who had come into the room, but undoubtedly the most beautiful girl he had ever seen in his life.

CHAPTER TWO

Spring came unexpectedly to Peking where, since it was so far North, it came later than in any other part of the country.

But now the almond trees were blossoming in the courtyard of Tseng-Wen's house, the magnolia was in bud and the pomegranate trees showed pink.

Stanton Ware could feel the sun warm on his face and the winds no longer had the chill of snow in them.

He knew that outside the City the Chinese landscape was now a delight, but he could see nothing beyond the confines of the courtyards in his host's house.

There the stone pools were filled with goldfish moving among the green leaves and wax-like flowers of the water lilies and flanked by artificially cultivated dwarf trees.

He was, however, fortunate in knowing what was going on in the outside world because Tseng-Wen had allotted to him a servant by the name of Yin.

This was surely one of the intelligent alert Chinese who conveyed secret information of everything that happened from the Forbidden City to the Lantern streets of the beggars and back to his Master.

Yin was the type of companion whom Stanton Ware had expected to take with him on his journey to Li Hung-Chang.

Even after a week of being the guest of Tseng-Wen he still could not believe that he was expected to have a woman to accompany him.

When she first entered Tseng-Wen's room and he looked at her incredulously, he had thought, and he had not changed his mind, that she was the most beautiful woman he had ever seen.

She was fully dressed in Chinese fashion, in the long straight satin coat embroidered with phoenixes and flowers, with trousers in the same silk peeping out above her pearl-decorated shoes.

But Stanton Ware's experience of the many nationalities comprised in China told him that she was not wholly Manchu.

Without looking at him she had walked across the room to kneel in front of Tseng-Wen in the prescribed manner and bow her head to the ground.

"You sent for me, Exalted One," she began.

She had a low and sweet musical voice that seemed to Stanton Ware to ripple through him and awoke an echo that made him think that he had heard it before.

Then he told himself he must be mistaken for if he had ever looked on such a beautiful face it would have been impossible to forget it.

"Rise, my precious child," Tseng-Wen said. "I wish you to meet Major Stanton Ware, the man I have spoken about."

Stanton Ware had naturally risen to his feet and now he bowed courteously, aware as he did so that the girl's acknowledgement was perfunctory and not as profound as might have been expected.

Addressing him, Tseng-Wen said,

"This is Perfect Pearl, the daughter of my heart and soul, although in fact we have no blood relationship in this life."

Stanton Ware knew that he spoke of previous reincarnations.

"Zivana, for that is her real name, is the daughter of Prince Vasili Kovanovich, whom I loved deeply in my youth."

He would have continued had not the girl interrupted him,

"Dare I question your wisdom, Most Noble One, in suggesting it is most unwise to trust a foreigner with our secrets?"

Tseng-Wen smiled.

"Have you forgotten, my child, that you are also a foreigner? And that your mother was English."

Her eyes blazed.

"I hate the English, as you well know! My mother was a Saint and her family repudiated her because she married my father."

"Nevertheless, you are your mother's daughter," Tseng-Wen insisted, "and your adopted country, China, needs your help. You must therefore work with Major Ware."

There was no mistaking the fiery look she gave him, Stanton Ware thought, and the way that her exquisitely curved lips tightened.

He knew that it was by sheer willpower that she prevented herself from expressing the defiant words that rose to her lips.

Because he had no wish to encumber himself with a woman, and certainly not a reluctant one, Stanton Ware said hastily,

"I bow to your wisdom, my Honourable Host, but perhas this lady speaks good sense when she suggests that, if she accompanies me on this mission, the dangers I encounter will be doubled."

Tseng-Wen smiled again.

"I have not finished my introduction," he said with just a touch of reproof in his voice. "Zivana may well have a Russian father and an English mother, but her grandmother was a Manchu Princess of the Royal House."

He paused for Stanton Ware to be impressed before he continued,

"She was brought up in the ways and customs of an Imperial Palace and will therefore be of the utmost assistance to you when you become the guest of Prince Tuan."

Stanton Ware looked doubtful and Zivana said almost scornfully,

"Do you really think that this Englishman could deceive the Prince or indeed the shrewd perception of Li Hung-Chang?"

Neither man spoke and she continued,

"The Viceroy has been to England and he has travelled in many parts of the world. He would notice an English characteristic, an English turn of phrase, which another man might miss."

"I am well aware of that," Tseng-Wen said quietly. "So it will be our duty, yours and mine, to prevent such slips and to ensure that Major Ware's mission is, if the Gods permit, successful."

Again Stanton Ware noticed that there was an expression of dislike in Zivana's beautiful eyes.

Never, he thought, had he seen eyes that were so expressive or so revealing. They were dark and yet they held strange lights that made them very unlike Chinese eyes.

And her hair was dark too, the deep raven's wing black that was the ultimate beauty of every Manchu.

Yet it held blue lights that gave her an unreal ethereal look, which was echoed by the pure translucent whiteness of her skin and the impression she gave of being so light and so slim as to be insubstantial.

She was indeed small for a Manchu rather than for a Chinese, who were tiny people.

The Manchu women, who had ridden at the side of their men and herded flocks in the harsh Northern landscape, originally had all been tall, strong and mountain-bred.

But their Royal Family was descended from the great Northern Emperors and those of the Royal blood were the most cultured and the most intelligent people in the whole of the Orient.

After two long centuries of colonising the Chinese, the Manchus had themselves been colonised.

The hardy tough-living archers, hunters and the warriors finally yielded to the spell of Chinese wisdom and Confucian pacifism.

Yet still living and breathing in them was a very proud spirit and in some a spiritual flame which remained unquenchable,

Looking at Zivana, Stanton Ware thought the combination of her blood had resulted in something so rare and exquisite that she was like a delicate porcelain vase, so thin that it was transparent.

He felt that he could see past her external beauty to an inner loveliness that he sensed with every nerve of his body.

And yet her dislike of him was very obvious.

"You know whatever you command me to do," she said to Tseng-Wen, "I will then do it because of my love for you. But I remain unconvinced that this foreigner can be the saviour of China."

"If he fails, there is no one else who we can put our trust in."

"I am flattered and honoured," Stanton Ware interposed. "At the same time let me add my plea to this lady's, I would rather visit Li Hung-Chang alone."

"It would seem strange for a Mandarin such as you will pretend to be, young vigorous and virile, to travel for so many miles without companionship. It would be customary for any such man to have a concubine with him and there is no one else that I would trust in such a position except for Zivana."

"A concubine?" Stanton Ware exclaimed almost incredulously.

Equally he realised that it was exactly what Li Hung-Chang and certainly Prince Tuan, would expect of him.

He thought quickly for some alternative.

But he knew that even the type of girl that Diverse Delight could provide for him from the 'House of a Thousand Joys' would be useless on a journey of such significance.

Such girls would certainly be of no help to him personally and it would be impossible to tell them the truth and let them learn that he was a foreigner.

As if aware of the thoughts going through his guest's mind, Tseng-Wen said,

"There is no time for further discussion. There is so much to be planned and so much to be learnt."

He turned to Zivana.

"You, my child, my sublime Precious Pearl, who I entrust with the safety of this man, you must instruct him, as I shall do, so that he is word-perfect before you both leave here."

The old Mandarin spoke with an authority Stanton Ware knew was decisive and there would be no further argument.

As if she realised it too, Zivana bent her lovely head in submission.

*

From that moment Stanton Ware felt as if he had been sent back to school.

There were four different ranks of Mandarins and their standing was proclaimed by the number of their retinue and outriders, the colour of their carriages, the button on their round caps and the *pu, tzu*, the embroidered plaque on their breasts.

The Mandarins of the first and second ranks wore green, the third and fourth blue, while Imperial yellow was reserved for the Son of Heaven and his retainers alone.

Tseng-Wen's friend was a Mandarin of the second rank and Stanton Ware's clothes were chosen accordingly and the button on top of his round cap was a coral, his plaque a golden pheasant.

He laughingly told Tseng-Wen that he was rather disappointed that he could not emulate General Gordon.

The hero of Khartoum had been in China and had been awarded, in recognition of his brilliant campaign against the Taipings, the highest honours. And he was known as 'Chinese Gordon'.

These consisted of the Yellow Riding Jacket and ruby button of the first rank.

But Tseng-Wen had merely answered,

"All in good time, my son. He who makes haste slowly is certain of arrival."

For two hours in the morning and two hours in the afternoon Stanton Ware had lessons in the Manchu language and in the customs and history of its people, a great deal of which he knew already.

He was sensible enough, however, to realise that one could always learn even more and he applied himself as diligently as any schoolboy.

He learnt the ceremonial approaches to those who were his equal, his superiors and their followers and servants.

Finally for two hours each and every day he talked with Zivana, learning from her many things about the women of China that he had not known before.

Because the weather was warm they sat outside in one of the courtyards.

He thought when she came to him wearing her exquisitely embroidered Chinese robes that she seemed to blend with the flowers and her beauty was a part of them.

But she spoke to him coldly and he knew she disliked him, although she never expressed her feelings in any way, but she was as impassive and inscrutable as any Chinese he had ever known.

Because he was to be a Mandarin it was so important, Tseng-Wen had told him, that he should know all about the Dowager Empress and the intrigues that were taking place in the Forbidden City.

When she spoke of the extravagance of the Dowager Empress, it was the first time since they had begun to talk together that Zivana's voice showed any emotion.

"In the country people are starving," she said. "They are over-taxed and it is hard for the ordinary Chinese to obtain any form of justice."

"How do you know all this this?" Stanton Ware asked.

"I have travelled a great deal," she answered him coldly, as if she resented his asking a personal question, and she went on,

"It is estimated that the annual upkeep of the Forbidden City is six and a half million pounds a year! And there are six thousand people living within its high walls."

"How can they spend so much?" Stanton Ware questioned.

"What has upset the people of the country more than anything is the way the Dowager Empress cheated the country to build herself a Summer Palace."

Stanton Ware had heard of this, but he asked as if he was ignorant,

"How did she do this?"

"I suppose the truth is that she has never forgotten the vanished Summer Palaces that had been destroyed, one of them by the British."

"And so she was determined to build another for herself," Stanton Ware prompted.

"One of the Ministers," Zivana said, "allowed the Empress to milk the funds allotted to the Admiralty Board and to divert huge sums intended for the construction of warships and desperately needed sea defences into her Privy Purse."

"It was disgraceful, but what might have been expected," Stanton Ware exclaimed.

"That was only the beginning of the money that was being spent by her and, of course, there are many other tales that have been told and told again until it is not surprising that the people will look anywhere, even to the Boxers, for leadership."

"What sort of tales?" he asked.

"Have you forgotten that the Old Buddha once shared the Regentship with Niuhura, her husband's Consort, and was then crowned Empress?"

"Naturally I do remember that."

"The very considerable jealousy between the two women after the Emperor's death was common knowledge and everybody understood what had happened when on one afternoon a eunuch presented Niuhura, as she gazed into the goldfish pool in the gardens, with a dish of milk cakes as a gift from her Co-Regent."

Stanton Ware smiled faintly, he knew the end of this story.

"Niuhura took a mouthful," Zivana went on, "and by the evening she was dead."

She looked at Stanton Ware warningly.

"I am telling you this story," she said, "to show you that if the Empress had the slightest idea that you had disguised yourself as a Mandarin, not only would your life be forfeit but also Tseng-Wen's, mine and every other person who lives in this house."

"I am aware of that," he said quietly.

She looked away from him and her profile was so perfect against the brilliant flowers of an azalea bush that he said impulsively,

"Whatever Tseng-Wen might say, let me go alone on this journey. No woman should be exposed to the risks that are part of my life and my career."

She did not answer and he went on,

"If I die, I die in a good cause."

"It is my cause too."

"But why? You are not wholly a Manchu and Russia only wishes to trade with China as England does. Forget the problems of the great Powers. Enjoy yourself as you should do at your age."

"Only the English speak of age as if it is of great importance," Zivana answered. "One is old or young, not in one's body but in one's mind."

Stanton Ware also believed that, but he answered her mockingly,

"I am sure you are a very old soul."

"That is what I believe and, although I am reluctant to admit it, I think that you also have lived many lives before this one."

"Reluctant?" he questioned with a smile.

"You know that I hate the English!"

"Quite unjustifiably for I feel you have not known many of them."

"My mother ran away with my father. He met her in England when he was attending a Court function with the Ambassador from St. Petersburg."

She stopped speaking and after a moment Stanton Ware said quietly,

"They fell in love?"

"Wildly and crazily," Zivana answered. "From that moment they had eyes only for each other."

"That is how love should be,"

"It is very Russian," she parried scornfully.

"And sometimes, only sometimes, I will grant you, very English," he said. "Go on with your story."

"They ran away together. My mother's father cut her out of his life as if she had never existed. It hurt her and she could not speak of it without tears until her dying day."

She looked at him and asked,

"Are you surprised that I hate your country and all its hard-hearted insensitive citizens?"

"Of which I am one!"

"Undoubtedly, although, according to Tseng-Wen, you have some virtues."

"How kind of you to acknowledge them," Stanton Ware retorted ironically.

"He has told me of the work you have done in China in the past and in other parts of the East. I suppose you look upon it as a game as amusing as hunting a fox or hitting a little ball about on the polo field."

There was no doubt that she was being sarcastic.

"Exactly," Stanton Ware replied. "A game at which one hopes to win, but one does not cry if one loses."

"It is what I expected," she said angrily, "and only a fool, Major Ware, plays carelessly with a loaded weapon."

"And only one who lacks self-control would wear his heart on his sleeve," Stanton Ware responded.

Because she knew, he rebuked her for being emotional, the colour burned in her cheeks and she rose from the cushioned seat where she had been sitting.

"I think we have done enough for today," she said.

"On the contrary, I have a great deal more I wish to hear. We have not discussed, and I think it important, the behaviour of concubines."

Zivana was still and he went on,

"As you will be acting in that role when we go on our journey, it is, I think, essential that I should know as much as possible about the concubines in Imperial service and those who attend such Dignitaries as Prince Tuan."

Ziyana realised that for the first time Stanton Ware was using his authority to make her obey his wishes.

She stood irresolute, wanting to leave him contemptuously at the same time feeling that she would lose face and give him a moral victory if she did so.

Reluctantly she sat down again and asked abruptly, although the sweetness of her voice made the words softer than she intended,

"What do you wish to know?"

"All that you know yourself."

He could see that she was hating him because he was compelling her against her will to continue talking with him.

Grudgingly she said,

"When a concubine, such as Tz'u-hsi, who is now the Dowager Empress, is called for service in The Palace, she joins the other Manchu girls sent for at the same time."

"How many?"

"About sixty. They wear the finest robes and jewels their families can buy or borrow and in procession they pass into the Imperial City and by the maze of halls, Pavilions, Temples, Pagodas and living quarters."

"They must find it very frightening."

"For a sixteen-year-old girl I should imagine it is terrifying," Zivana answered. "Inside the walls the concubines-elect exchange their servants for Palace eunuchs, then they proceed on foot across a wide courtyard and up a flight of white marble stairs."

Stanton Ware could visualise it, knowing they would see the vermilion up-tilted Temples of the Tutelary Gods and the Imperial Ancestors.

Every building they looked at would be ablaze with colour, guarded against evil spirits, by snarling, grotesque lion-dogs and tortoises.

"The Manchu girls are escorted ceremoniously across the Golden Water River," Zivana went on. "Then in Tz'u-hsi's day she and the others met the Emperor's stepmother, who was accompanied by the Chief Eunuch.

"The five lucky characters of her birth that formed her horoscope were examined and all the girls were inspected for blemishes, defects and other illnesses before finally they joined a household that already numbered six thousand people."

'A frightening prospect on its own,' Stanton Ware reflected,

"That is true, but what must be even more frightening is that a concubine faces months and perhaps even years of loneliness and isolation when she never sees the Emperor and in fact never sets eyes on a man except for the eunuchs."

Zivana paused for a moment and then she carried on,

"I have learnt from someone who knew Tz'u-hsi when she was a girl that the Emperor, who was later to be her husband, would often slip out of the Forbidden City with some of his favourite eunuchs."

"Where would he go?"

"He would visit the dives of the Outer City, frequent its Flower Houses, opium dens, observe peepshows, watch the dancers and above all to consort with its forbidden 'lily-foot' Chinese women."

Stanton Ware listened but made no remark.

He was only surprised that someone quite so young as Zivana should know all this even though he knew it himself.

But he realised that such behaviour would be known only too well to the men with whom he would associate and therefore he continued to listen.

"My informant told me," Zivana went on, "that one day the Chief Eunuch turned over the jade tablet on which the

Emperor wrote the name of the concubine he wanted to sleep with that night and he found Tz'u-hsi's name inscribed."

"How long had she then been in the Forbidden City?" Stanton Ware asked.

"Three years. Now the Chief Eunuch went to her apartments, undressed her, wrapped her in a scarlet rug and carried her on his shoulder to the Emperor's bed.

"It was the first time she had seen him and etiquette required that she should crawl up from the foot of the bed towards the Emperor."

"A position of utmost humility," Stanton Ware murmured.

"At dawn," Zivana went on, "the Chief Eunuch gathered Tz'u-hsi up again and carried her back to her rooms. The day that she had visited the Emperor was written in a book and authenticated with his seal."

"It is strange and in England we would say it was a barbaric ceremony," Stanton Ware remarked.

"I have heard that Englishwomen think they are the equals of men or, worse still, their superiors."

"And what else have you heard?" he asked with a smile.

"The grand ladies, because they are beautiful, order men about, who, being spineless and weak, obey."

Stanton Ware smiled at the contempt in her voice.

"Whom do you despise more," he asked, "a woman who gives orders, and who gives more than the Dowager Empress, or a man who obeys them?"

"I think they are both wrong," Zivana answered. "A man is born to rule and command. If we did not have an Emperor who is weak enough to be imprisoned by his aunt, we would not be in the position that we are at the moment."

"Perhaps you are right," he said, "but many men are so weak because the wrong sort of women have had the wrong influence on them."

"A man who is a man should be strong, not only physically but also mentally. A woman should inspire but never order him about."

Stanton Ware laughed and, when Zivana turned to look at him in surprise, he explained,

"I was just wondering which part of your blood put such words into your mouth."

"Can I not think for myself?"

"No," he answered, "you are blown about by three winds, a Chinese wind that thinks you should be submissive and bow low before your Lord and Master and a Russian wind, which makes you feel fiery, tempestuous and ready to defy the all-conquering male, yet you glory in his power over you."

He saw Zivana's eyes flutter as if she wished to refute what he was saying, but before she could speak, he continued,

"Thirdly there is the English wind which tells you that love can be something so perfect between two people who are equal because they were made for each other. Then it is not a question of conquering or being conquered but of union."

There was silence before Zivana said in a very low voice,

"That is what my father and mother found together."

"And that is what you hope to find as well?"

"I am Manchu. When I came here to this household to live with Tseng-Wen because my father trusted him more than anybody he knew in Russia, I vowed myself to the service of China."

She looked at Stanton Ware as if she challenged him and went on,

"I studied and learnt as I knew that for this wonderful country there were troublesome times ahead."

She paused before she added in a different tone,

"It was part of my Karma. There were certain things that I must do to erase past mistakes or pay debts from previous lives."

Her voice ceased and after a moment Stanton Ware said,

"I think you have already done things that have been of assistance, but neither you nor Tseng-Wen have told me about them."

"They are not important, they were small ways I could help because I had an entrée not only to the Forbidden City but also to the Russian Legation."

"While you ignored the British," Stanton Ware remarked.

"I have no wish to help the British."

"But now, perhaps through Fate that was written in your Karma, you have to help me."

"As I have told you, I am Manchu. I obey my spiritual father, Tseng-Wen, and accept his wisdom."

"Perhaps this assignment, or whatever you may call it, may not be as unpleasant as you anticipate."

"I did not say it would be unpleasant. All work, if it concerns the future of China, is something that I am prepared to give my whole mind and heart to."

"But you would rather not work with me."

"I did not say so."

"I saw in your eyes what you thought and I can still read very clearly what you think."

Her dark eyelashes fluttered against her pale cheeks and he knew she was embarrassed and a little shy at the thought that he was so perceptive.

"Because it is Tseng-Wen's wish," she said, "I shall do and say what you expect of me."

"I should expect any concubine who looked to me for protection to give me not only obedience but sympathy and understanding," Stanton Ware pointed out.

As he spoke, he thought of Diverse Delight and the way her girls were trained to make each man they associated with believe, if only for one evening, that he was to her the most important person in the world.

Zivana looked startled and he knew that what he had suggested was a revolutionary idea that had not occurred to her.

"So you must think of it like this," Stanton Ware said. "The men against whom we are pitting our brains are very astute and many of them have been trained in the esoteric sciences, which give them an awareness that exceeds that of the average human being.

"They will try to look deep into my mind and to find out not whether I am speaking the truth but whether I am thinking it."

He looked at her searchingly as he continued,

"They will undoubtedly do the same with you for the way of knowledge very often lies in a woman's hands."

"I had not – thought of that," Zivana murmured.

"That is why, if we are to be successful and if our disguise is to go undetected, we must work together in perfect harmony," he said. "If you give me mere lip-service, I cannot help thinking that those who watch us – and make no mistake, they are very astute – will realise you are not what you pretend to be."

As if it agitated her, Zivana rose from the cushioned seat to walk across the courtyard to stare down at the goldfish moving beneath the green leaves of the water lilies.

A little fountain springing from the mouth of a dolphin threw its water iridescent like a thousand rainbows up into the sky where it fell again with a soft tinkle into the carved basin beneath it.

Zivana's body was very slight, silhouetted against the grey stones.

Her dark head with its skilfully arranged hair held by jewelled pins seemed almost too large for the delicate column of her long neck.

For a long time she stood looking down into the water and Stanton Ware knew that she was peering into her own soul.

Then she turned and came back to him.

"I have been wrong," she said softly. "I have let prejudice influence my judgement and so I must apologise."

She raised her eyes and he saw that she was speaking in all sincerity.

"I will not have you apologise," he said, "for as far as I am concerned you have done nothing wrong. But I would ask of you that you believe, as I do, that peace for China is more important than any personal feelings."

"You are right – of course you are right," Zivana murmured.

"I fell in love with China many years ago when I first came here," Stanton Ware said. "I know her faults, but I also know her potential greatness."

His voice deepened as he went on,

"Beneath the surface of all the things we have talked of today, the poverty, the cruelty and the wrong leadership, there is the wisdom of ages and the stirring of a light that will one day illuminate the whole world."

"You believe – you really believe that?" Zivana asked breathlessly.

"I believe, but I know as well that, when a seed is planted in the ground, it is a long time before it becomes a great tree."

He sighed.

"China has to go through many experiences before eventually she will find herself. But the legends tell us that one day she will be overwhelmingly powerful and her philosophy will rule the whole world."

He smiled as if to take away the seriousness of his words and added,

"You and I will not be there to see it, for what is a hundred, a thousand or even tens of thousands of years in the Wheel of Eternity?"

"In the meantime China will suffer."

"Mostly through her own fault," Stanton Ware said, "and if it is you and I, Zivana, who must try to correct things, we may be very small cogs in a very big wheel."

He smiled before he continued,

"But just as a grain of sand can bring a large machine to a standstill or a drop of oil make it work faster, who knows how important we may be each of us to this vast Empire?"

"You are right!" Zivana cried. "Forgive me for the hard things I have – thought about you and for my – attitude until now."

She sounded so contrite and her eyes looking up into his urged him to understand.

"If there has been any misunderstanding," Stanton Ware said, "it is now forgotten."

"You are very generous."

"No, only anxious that what we do together, and I believe there is a great deal for us to do, shall be undertaken without reserve on either side."

"There will be none as far as I am concerned – that I promise," Zivana said.

"Then I am certain that insofar as it is possible to do so we shall succeed."

He looked into her eyes for a long moment and then he lifted her hand and kissed it.

*

The following day Yin and Zivana discussed his appearance with Stanton Ware.

His clothes had returned from the tailor and he looked at them with interest, knowing that every piece of embroidery and every button had a special significance that was important for him to remember.

He knew that the first thing he had to do was to shave his head and wear a queue.

When the Manchus conquered China in 1644 they at once ordered their new subjects to shave their heads, leaving the queue or pigtail to grow from the crown as a symbol of their submission to Ch'ing rule.

From that day all males over the age of fourteen were forced to adopt the style and the queue often reached their knees.

It actually had a powerful image.

It stereotyped the Chinaman for many centuries in the West and even inspired General Washington and King George III to wear docked versions of it.

In China its importance as a symbol of subjection continued despite protests.

The Taiping rebels of the 1850s and1 860s, when Tz'u-hsi was first Empress, wore their hair wild and loose, but the majority of Chinamen conformed because they were too weak to do otherwise.

The Manchu costume for men and women was a loose coat fastened at the side, worn over a tunic and pantaloons.

It was embroidered with flowers and animals, emblems and symbolic birds.

It was also studded with as many precious stones, pearls, and gold as its owner could buy.

By their own decree the Manchus always remained foreigners in China.

In a population of four hundred million there were only five million Manchus, but they held all the most consequential civil positions.

Dressed as a Mandarin, Stanton Ware looked very impressive and Yin shaved his head to the crown and with considerable cunning joined a queue of false hair to his own at the back.

It gave him, Stanton Ware thought, a very strange appearance, but he supposed he would grow used to it and because at first he felt a little self-conscious he was happy to wear his Mandarin hat on all possible occasions.

He wondered how Zivana and he could disguise their eyes, although he was aware that the slanting eyes, which the West expected every Chinese person to have, had in fact little to do with the Manchus.

The Manchu type, especially in high-bred women, was very near to the European. Their noses were straight, their eyes had no Chinese slant and they looked out straight and clear under black brows.

He knew that many of the ladies of the Legations were surprised when they first saw the Dowager Empress, realising that her eyes looked like their own and did not slant up at the corners as they had expected.

"At the same time," Zivana said, "because it is wise to let people see what they want to see, Yin and I have a special gum from a recipe that has been handed down through many generations. It will make your eyelids and mine completely smooth and just extend a little at the corners."

She demonstrated as she spoke and Stanton Ware realised that, with his shaved head and heavy-lidded eyes, it would be hard for anyone to suspect him of not being a Manchu,

"Do you have to wear the traditional make-up on your face?" he asked.

He thought as he spoke that it would be a crime to cover her perfect skin with the thick white mask with which the majority of both Chinese and Manchu women disguised their dark complexions.

Zivana shook her head.

"A little powder is all I shall need," she answered. "The white paste contains lead and is therefore dangerous."

"I have heard that," Stanton Ware answered.

He thought as he spoke that Zivana was so lucky that she did not have to trouble herself with having bound feet.

Manchu women had never bound their feet like the sheltered Chinese.

From the age of five or six, bandages were bound tightly round the feet of a Chinese girl, forcing the heel under the instep to meet the crumpled toes and make the whole foot measure not more than three inches in length.

In her tiny embroidered shoes with the beri-boned pantaloons falling over swollen and deformed ankles, the Chinese girl minced along on the arm of one of her servants.

This was the famous 'lily-walk', as the undulating of her figure as she tottered on her crippled feet was extolled in prose and verse.

When the bandages were removed, the bad smell of compressed flesh was appalling, but bound feet were not only thought to be seductive but had become through the ages a symbol of caste.

Naturally the peasants and coolies just could not afford to immobilise their daughters, because they needed their labour.

But the upper-class Chinese gloried in their superiority and Manchu women often longed to adopt the exotic deformation that denoted an exclusive status.

Fortunately foot-binding was strictly against Manchu laws and traditions.

There was therefore no difficulty where Zivana was concerned in that her feet, small in themselves, could remain exactly as God had intended them to be.

At the end of the week Stanton Ware was becoming restless and wondering how long he would have to go on hiding himself in Tseng-Wen's house.

Comfortable though it was, he longed to be outside and encountering some sort of action.

Then Yin came back with news that Li Hung-Chang was expected to arrive at The Palace of Prince Tuan within the next two days.

"That means we can start at once!" Stanton Ware exclaimed eagerly.

Tseng-Wen nodded.

"Tomorrow everything will be ready for you to leave as soon as the sun has risen fully in the Heavens."

Stanton Ware gave a sigh of relief.

"You will understand, most generous of hosts, if I say I am glad."

"I do understand and I think too it is important that there should be no delay."

There was a note in the old man's voice that made Stanton Ware glance at him sharply.

In answer without words he put into his hand a placard.

"Yin brought this back from the Chinese City," he said. "It was displayed in a prominent place."

Stanton Ware looked at it and realised at once that it was a product of the Boxers.

Written in Chinese, it said,

"So as soon as the practice of the Ho Ch'uan has been brought to perfection — wait for three times three or nine times nine, nine times nine or three times three — then shall the devils meet their doom. The will of Heaven is that the telegraph wires be first cut, then the railways torn up and then shall the foreign devils be decapitated. In this day shall the hour of their calamities come. The time for rain to fall is yet afar off and all on account of the devils."

Stanton Ware's lips tightened as he read it.

"Yin said that there were great crowds staring at it," Tseng-Wen remarked.

Stanton Ware looked at him.

"Shall we be too late?" he asked.

The old man merely made a gesture with his hands.

"Time always lies in the lap of the Gods," he answered, "and you could not move sooner for Li Hung-Chang was not there, but now he will be and you can only do your best."

"That is undoubtedly true," Stanton Ware agreed. "Zivana and I can only do our best!"

CHAPTER THREE

As they drove out of the Imperial City, Stanton Ware thought that he had been correct in thinking that the countryside would be beautiful with the coming of spring.

The ground was thick with the white blossoms of the wild wood-jasmine, which had a scent almost like that of tuberoses.

The mimosa was a spray of powdery gold, which made the trees a glory that rivalled the sun.

They were moving slowly over the uneven roads in a carriage drawn by four horses that Tseng-Wen had supplied them with.

It was the sort of carriage which would have been looked upon with disdain by all the foreigners who had brought to their Legations well-sprung European chaises in which they travelled about at what seemed to the Chinese to be a frightening speed.

But Tseng-Wen had briefed Stanton Ware very thoroughly before they left.

He was told that the carriage they travelled in and which in some ways looked more like a cart, was the exact type of old-fashioned vehicle that would be owned by a Mandarin who came from the mountains of Shansi.

"You have come to Peking very slowly and over excruciatingly bad roads," Tseng-Wen explained. "There while you rested you changed horses and servants."

Stanton Ware knew that this was important for the servants who had been chosen for him by Tseng-Wen had therefore no idea of his movements previous to their engagement.

There were sixteen of them.

Some travelled behind in another green cart, others rode shaggy Mogul horses.

For a Mandarin of the first rank there would have been at least twenty, while the Son of Heaven when he went abroad in his palanquin had no less than sixty attendants in front and behind him.

Zivana sat beside Stanton Ware on a seat covered with silk cushions and he thought as he looked at her that she appeared even more beautiful than she had before.

Her silk coat was of pigeons-blood red, embroidered with magnolias and over it she wore in case she was cold a cloak lined with rich Russian sable.

Her blue-black hair was swept up on top of her head and the jewelled hairpins in it were he knew worth a fortune.

They glittered as she moved, as did protectors over her long nails, which made her small white hands look excessively fragile and helpless.

They drove for a little while without speaking.

Then, as Stanton Ware drew aside the curtains on his side of the carriage to look out at the almond-blossom trees, she said,

"Would you think it impertinent if I asked where you went last night?"

He turned his head to smile at her.

"I thought we agreed that we would have no secrets from each other."

"None?"

"None as far as I am concerned," he replied, "and so I intended to inform you of what I learnt when I went to the American Legation."

"The American?" she exclaimed in surprise.

"The reason that I did so is that it is hopeless to speak to the British Minister, Sir Claude Macdonald. He is still convinced that everything that anyone has told him about the Boxers is exaggerated and of little consequence."

"And you thought that the Americans might be more understanding?"

"Not the Minister, a man called 'Clobber'. He is of the same mind as Sir Claude and they both imagine that their flags will protect them whatever trouble arises."

"Then who did you speak to?"

"The First Secretary, Herbert Squiers."

Zivana laughed.

"The Americans have such funny names!"

"They think the Chinese ones much funnier and far more difficult to remember."

"I am rebuked. What did Mr. Herbert Squiers have to say?"

"He is a sensible man who told me that he had seen trouble coming for a long time and I promised that, when I had some news, I would get in touch with him."

"You can trust him?"

"Implicitly!"

Zivana gave a little sigh.

"Then that is one more person we can count on."

Stanton Ware had already told her just how stupid and obstinate the British Minister had been and she had the same impression where the Russians were concerned.

She had been in touch with the Russian Legation, but so like the British they had pooh-poohed her warnings and been certain that the Boxers were just an unruly rabble that could be dispersed quite easily should the need arise.

Stanton Ware had shown Herbert Squiers the placard that had been shown in the Chinese City.

He had promised to bring it to the attention of his Minister, but he was quite certain it would not be taken seriously.

"In my opinion," Stanton Ware had said before he left the Legation, "you are living in a Fool's Paradise."

"I totally agree with you," Herbert Squiers had replied. "But as long as our Ministers are concerned only with their Race Meetings, with bridge parties and entertaining each other, the reports from the Provinces go unread on their desks."

"Let us hope that you and I, Mr. Squiers, are just worrying unnecessarily," Stanton Ware said.

Even as he spoke he knew that it was a vain hope.

Wearing Manchu clothes but not dressed as a Mandarin, he had walked back through the Chinese City, noticing that many of the teeming crowds were ragged, squalid and diseased.

Even some of the Officials' resplendent robes were in need of replacement and Stanton Ware thought that this was just the sort of ground on which the Boxers could sow the seeds of revolution.

The streets too were dirty and night-soil merchants were busy collecting manure, both human and animal, parsimoniously in jars to carry it away to the country.

It was all sordid and down-at-heel and only as he moved towards the Forbidden City was everything changed,

Through the green foliage of the trees coming into bud there was the gleaming gold of the Imperial yellow tiles, the bright enamel of the Temple roofs and an explosion of scarlet, emerald and azure on the Pavilions with their ornate upturned eaves.

He recalled Zivana's tales of the extravagances that took place in the Forbidden City.

As he saw women and children searching the gutters for waste from better-class houses and scraps of bread, he wondered how not only the Legations but also the Empress and those who ruled with her could be so blind.

He told Zivana what he had seen and he knew that it hurt her to think of the suffering of the ordinary Chinese people.

He wondered how many women, brought up as she had been in the luxury and comfort of Palaces and in houses like the one owned by Tseng-Wen would be concerned with those less fortunate than themselves.

"Are you nervous?" he asked as they journeyed on.

She gave him a smile and he noticed that her eyes, now that she had used the special gum on them, were half-crescents of darkness and mystery.

"Not exactly nervous," she replied, "but breathless with expectation, like waiting for the curtain to go up in the theatre. One knows that one will see a play, but, until it begins, you are not certain what it will be about."

"The Chinese refer to it," Stanton Ware said, "as 'drawing in breath before the leap'."

"How I do love the Chinese way of explaining things!" Zivana exclaimed. "When I am worried or afraid, I remember that Confucius said, '*It is man who can make the Way great*'."

"Or woman," Stanton Ware added softly.

"Have you forgotten that I am only an accessory? This is your expedition not mine."

"And yet, as you know, Tseng-Wen thinks that I cannot do without you."

"I hope you will be able to say that when it is all over."

"I am sure I shall, but we must not boast. It might be unlucky," Stanton Ware said with a smile. "Must we be as superstitious as the Empress? "Why not? In China we should do as the Chinese do. Every one of your people from the Empress down to the lowest coolie believes in astrology, fortune-tellers, clairvoyants and augurers, who are consulted on everything."

Zivana gave a little laugh.

"We should have consulted one before we left."

"Do you mean to say you did not do so?" he asked her half-seriously.

She looked away from him, shyly and then said,

"I am certain that Tseng-Wen did so on our behalf. That is why he was insistent that we should leave at the exact hour and the exact minute and neither earlier nor later."

Stanton Ware laughed in genuine amusement.

At the same time, he knew that no one could live in China and not be affected by its almost blind faith in the supernatural.

It had in fact been a brilliant move on the part of the Boxers to bedazzle people with their magic powers.

They drove until it was twelve o'clock and the sun was now high in the sky and then they stopped in a shady valley.

Yin, who was in charge of the servants, found a place under some pine trees where there was a little stream trickling beneath them and the ground was brilliant with spring flowers.

Cushions were brought from the carriages and a small table was set in front of them from which they could eat.

The Samshu wine was cooled in the stream and the food was very rich and exotic as the servants would expect a Mandarin to enjoy.

There was bread baked in moulds shaped like butterflies and there were Chinese dishes, which Stanton Ware had always enjoyed, but more so since he had stayed with Tseng-Wen.

Slivers of duck and pork, all with their special exotic sauces, were served, there were small melons stuffed with fruit and seeds, and ham and chicken which had been steamed for hours.

For Zivana, who drank very little of the fiery Chinese wine, there was tea flavoured with honeysuckle in an exquisite china teapot that fitted into its own padded basket.

When Yin had waited on them, he withdrew out of sight to join the other servants, who were eating their own repast.

Stanton Ware rose from his cushioned seat to sit cross-legged with his back against a silver pine tree.

"You have studied Yoga?" Zivana asked him suddenly.

He nodded.

"I had no idea."

"Is it important?"

"Very, to me. I have always longed to go to one of the Lamaseries to talk with the Lamas and have the chance to learn the Ancient Wisdom, but – "

She made a little gesture with her hands.

"I am only a woman "

"And a very attractive one, if I may say so," Stanton Ware replied.

She looked at him suspiciously, as if she thought he was paying her a mere compliment and then she laughed.

"*Manners maketh man,* as the English say. *And clothes maketh woman.*"

"I wonder what you would look like in European dress," Stanton Ware said reflectively. "I cannot help feeling it might be disappointing."

"You are not very flattering after all," Zivana replied mockingly.

Stanton Ware knew that her satin garments, the jewels in her hair and on her fingers and the vivid colours gave her an indescribable glamour and allure.

Perhaps, he then thought, it would all be lost in the froth and frills that gave the women of England, with their pinched-in waists, an hour-glass silhouette.

There was something so exquisite and exotic about Zivana, he decided, that she looked like a precious jewel to be put in a glass case and to be admired but never touched.

"Perfect Pearl," he said aloud, "I cannot imagine a better description."

For the first time since he had known her she looked self-conscious.

"I think it is time we should be moving on," she said.

He told himself that he had no wish to embarrass her.

While it was nothing new for him to travel with a female companion, although not on a mission as dangerous as this, for her it was obviously the first time.

He knew no other young girl would have ever accepted such a situation without being infuriatingly coy.

But Zivana had an almost masculine detachment except that she had hated him because of his nationality.

Never for one moment in all the time they had been together had she deliberately drawn attention to herself as a woman.

Nor had she invited him to think of her as anything but a colleague in their joint mission.

'She is unique,' Stanton Ware told himself.

As he watched her moving back under the silver pines to where the carriage was waiting for them, he thought again that her beauty was almost blinding.

They journeyed on and the first night they slept in tents under the trees in a small wood.

The inns in China were usually filthy noisy places and Stanton Ware had stayed in too many off the beaten track not to know that one not only encountered discomfort but risked robbery and worse.

The tents that Tseng-Wen had provided were roomy and when they had been set up with carpets on the floor, a cushioned couch and even small pieces of light furniture, no traveller could have asked for anything better.

They were now some way from Peking and they passed strings of camels that had been left by the frowning pyramidal gates for the wilds and there were Chinese traders with bland enigmatic faces and greedy souls.

"They are blood-suckers of the simple people," Zivana said, "and I hate them because they take away a man's savings and give him paper rubbish in return."

"Better pick a man's pocket than steal his soul," Stanton Ware quoted.

She smiled, but he knew that she spoke the truth and the simple lives of the coolies and peasants could be ruined by those who preyed upon their vanity and superstitions.

Nothing enjoyed larger sales in China than charms against sickness and death, charms for love, for birth, for money and for a good life which never came.

Also on the road were horse caravans carrying every sort of goods from the great mart of the Far East.

It was impossible not to think that if only the Dowager Empress and her advisors would realise how really important trading and open Ports were to China, it would be a rich and very prosperous country.

They came to a small village and, as they were passing through it, they then saw a great crowd gathered in the open marketplace.

Stanton Ware and Zivana were both looking through the window of the carriage and almost at the same moment they exclaimed,

"Boxers!"

They had seen the red scarves on their heads and the red bands around their wrists and ankles which the youths wore.

Because he was extremely interested to see what was happening, Stanton Ware called to the coachman to stop the horses.

As Manchu travellers they were quite safe and even the Boxers would not dare to insult a Mandarin.

The people in the village were all clustered round a boy who in the centre of a circle was kneeling with his eyes closed.

He folded his hands and began chanting, then he drew figures and cabalistic signs in the dust and sang chants to evoke the spirits.

He worked himself up into a frenzy, his gestures growing wilder and still wilder, his expression more and more exalted, his utterances more excited.

One of his companions came in front of him to ask,

"Who are you and what do you want?"

The boy's voice came as if from a long distance,

"I am – a great man – of history – a hero of – China's past."

He swayed backwards and forwards, his eyes closed.

"What do you want? What can we give you?" his companion asked.

"I want – a big sword – a sword in my hand."

"What will you do with your sword?"

He put out his hand and one of the people in the crowd came forward to hand him an ancient and rusty one.

Rising, still chanting, he began to thrust and parry, weave and plunge with the sword.

He was shadow-fighting. Then, as the people watched him, moved by his excitement and by his exhilaration, he shouted,

"Uphold the great Pure Dynasty and Exterminate the Barbarian!"

There was a wild shout of excitement at this.

Then, as he sank onto the ground exhausted, another member of his gang began dancing with wild contortions, calling on his companions to strike him.

Like Baldur the Beautiful, the Chinese hero, he stood in a trance before them.

They hit him with sticks and with the blade of the sword that the other boy had used.

Then, as he went on dancing, his companions produced a bow and arrow and the crowd screamed as an arrow struck him in the chest. Yet because he was in a deep trance it did not hurt him.

By this time the simple people of the village were entirely captivated.

"How is it possible, how can it happen that this boy is unhurt and still alive after all you have done to him?" one of them asked.

An older lad answered,

"We are invulnerable! Join us and you too will have such Heaven-sent Powers."

He climbed up onto a step to speak to the people, roaring out what he had to say in a loud voice.

"Heaven is angry with the foreigner and all his works and particularly with his religion – Christianity. We have come to purge China of this venom. For too long have we suffered from these foreign devils and, if there are Christian converts here in your village, you must be rid of them quickly! The Churches which belong to them must be burnt down. Burn, *burn*! Kill, *kill*!"

The shout became infectious and now the villagers began to echo him,

"Burn, *burn*! Kill, *kill!*"

Stanton Ware thought that it was getting out of hand and he signalled to his servants that they should move on. As they drove away they could still hear the voices echoing after them.

"Burn, *burn*! Kill, *kill!*"

"It is – frightening!" Zivana said at length in a low voice.

"But they will get many adherents, there is no doubt about that," Stanton Ware answered dryly.

"Before they leave," Zivana said, "Yin tells me that they will hand out tracts that include crazy recipes to ward off the poison they say that the foreigners have poured down the wells. They also contain charms and prayers against the evil of the Christians."

"They are surprisingly near to Peking," Stanton Ware said, "Surely the Empress must realise that when they are as far North as this, they might constitute a danger even to her?"

"I doubt it," Zivana replied. "Tseng-Wen is right when he says the Empress herself hates the foreigners and will use any weapon to be rid of them."

"There have been riots before, in fact two years ago," Stanton Ware said, "but then the Empress gave in and suppressed the rioters."

Zivana sighed.

"I have a feeling that she will not do so now."

They drove on for about two miles, then at another village once again there were Boxers.

This time there were no demonstrations, but ragged youths with red scarves and sashes were lounging about and there were posters and placards everywhere.

As they passed on, Stanton Ware was frowning.

The sun was beginning to sink behind the Western Mountains when they then saw in the distance rising above the trees the green roofs of Prince Tuan's Palace.

Stanton Ware turned and smiled at Zivana.

"Now the game begins," he said quietly.

He knew despite what she had said that she was nervous and so he added,

"We must be very careful of what we say to each other from now on."

"Tseng-Wen has told me," Zivana answered, "that we must always behave as if someone was listening, which doubtless they are, and that to converse in any language except Manchu would be disastrous."

"We will find a way if it is absolutely necessary," Stanton Ware said lightly.

They drove on and entered a well-cared-for Park, which gave way to exquisite gardens rich in colour surrounding The Palace.

Stanton Ware had already sent a servant ahead with his card to introduce himself and ask if he might have the privilege of meeting His Highness.

Hospitality in China was always open-handed and it would have been impossible for the Prince to refuse such a request even if he had wished to do so.

It was therefore not surprising that, as soon as their carriage drew up outside The Palace, a number of servants came hurrying down to help Stanton Ware alight.

As was correct, Zivana did not follow him from the carriage, but remained inside it to be taken round to another door of The Palace and she was then taken to the women's quarters.

Prince Tuan was an evil-visaged man of about forty, his face marked with smallpox scars and his eyes small and ferret-like.

Stanton Ware knew that he must be on his guard and that Tseng-Wen had been right in warning him that the Prince was untrustworthy.

He was the grandson of the Tao-Kuang Emperor and in Peking he wore the resplendent Manchu Military uniform of lacquered leather with eighteen sable tassels dangling from his jewel-encrusted helmet.

Because he was determined, thrusting and confident, he had caught the elderly eye of the Empress.

Since the Emperor had not produced a son, he had been clever enough to persuade her into appointing his own adolescent son, P'u-chun, as Heir Apparent to the Throne.

He also played on her superstitious fears and saw that she was deeply disturbed by the Boxers' claims to invulnerability.

Prince Tuan was, however, exceedingly affable, addressing his guest in the most flowery language and leading him into a room where Li Hung-Chang was waiting.

The Viceroy looked older than his years and he had in fact shrunk with age. His height, which had always made him seem impressive, was now lost because of his bowed shoulders.

His hair was white and his beard sparse. But there was still a flicker of youth in his eyes.

He spoke firmly with an authority that might have been expected from his achievements and the many positions he had held during the long years of his service to his country.

When the wine was brought, the three men sat around exchanging pleasantries and, as Tseng-Wen had told Stanton Ware to do, he explained his long journey from his native Shansi to Peking and told them that night he was returning home.

"And what did you think of Peking?" Li Hung-Chang enquired.

"It depressed me greatly," Stanton Ware answered.

"Depressed you?"

"I felt that there was a great apathy, which I had not expected, having heard even in the mountains where I live of the dangers that beset our beloved country."

"What danger?" Prince Tuan asked loudly.

"On my way here in a small village I saw the Boxers at work," Stanton Ware replied.

He knew by the expression in Li Hung-Chang's eyes that he was listening and the Prince said loudly,

"Gangs of ragged beggars extorting money from the peasants for charms, what harm can they do?"

"They were recruiting among the people as I understand they have been doing all over the country," Stanton Ware replied, "but especially in Shantung and Chihli."

"Secret Societies have existed in China for centuries," the Prince snapped, "and served many purposes. They have been wiped out time after time by the authorities in Peking, but they have always come back."

"I could not help feeling, Your Highness, although, of course, I may be wrong," Stanton Ware said, "that the Boxers are rather larger in number and more aggressive than the Secret Societies of the past."

The Prince did not answer, but Li Hung-Chang said,

"You actually saw a gang of Boxers between here and Peking?"

"Forty to fifty of them," Stanton Ware answered. "But by now they may have recruited many more from the village they were performing in. There were others and many posters in places we passed through."

Li Hung-Chang looked pensive.

"I did not know that they had come so far North, although I have heard that there has been trouble at Kaolo."

"What happened there?" Stanton Ware enquired.

"The report that reached me this morning from one of my own people," Li Hung-Chang replied, "was that a number of houses belonging to Christian Chinese have been burnt and many Christians killed."

The Prince did not speak and Li Hung-Chang went on,

"There was a clash between troops and Boxers in the Chihli Province as I passed through it. The Governor, who is weak, has allowed the movement to grow and there is a great deal of unrest."

"The Ho Ch'uan can easily be put down if it gets out of hand," the Prince remarked with deliberate casualness.

"The Boxers learnt in the Shantung Province that they had nothing at all to fear from the Dowager Empress," Li

Hung-Chang replied. "Every time the Governor informed her that he was going to pursue the Boxers and break them up, the Empress then gave out a new Imperial edict ordering him to go slow in his campaign and 'to reason with them'."

"The Old Buddha is wise," the Prince said. "She needs all the manpower she can get and it does not matter where it comes from."

"Are you seriously suggesting that these ragamuffin Boxers should be recruited into the Imperial Army?" Li Hung-Chang asked.

"Why not?" the Prince replied. "We are not strong enough without more men to fight for us."

Stanton Ware longed to ask the pertinent question – 'strong enough for what?'

But he knew the answer and was well aware without it being expressed in words that The Prince was violently anti-foreigner.

They then changed the subject and talked about the Prince's treasures which ornamented The Palace.

They also discussed a new book that had just been published on Confucianism, which very fortunately Stanton Ware had read and so could take part in the exchange of views that. Confucianism extolled the universal virtues of wisdom, humanity and courage.

He knew that Li Hung-Chang exemplified the first and the third virtues, but he was not certain about his humanity.

There was something autocratic and imperious about him and Stanton Ware wondered if at any time he had been really touched and distressed by the plight of the Chinese people.

He was not a Manchu, he was a Han-Chinese and yet it was hard to discover if he had ever tried to improve the lot of the poor even while he had been far-seeing enough to know that progress was essential for prosperity.

It was very near the time of their evening meal and the Prince said,

"I have a suggestion to make which I hope you gentlemen will approve of. After we have eaten, my concubines would be greatly honoured if they might entertain you."

"It sounds a pleasant way of passing the evening," Li Hung-Chang replied courteously.

The Prince looked at Stanton Ware.

"And you, Noble Sir," he said, "have brought with you, I believe, your own concubine. I hope that she too will join us."

Stanton Ware bowed and, because he had no alternative, said,

"If Perfect Pearl is not too tired after the journey, I am sure she would be very gratified by Your Highness's invitation."

It left Zivana a loophole by which she could refuse, but he had a feeling that she would not avail herself of it.

Sure enough, after their meal, a very long and delicious one, throughout which the wine flowed copiously, the concubines then came into the room where the three men were sitting at their ease on comfortable couches.

There were the three concubines belonging to the Prince and Zivana followed them.

All four girls knelt on entering the room and then bowed until their foreheads touched the floor.

Then they rose and Stanton Ware saw that, as the Prince's concubines were extremely attractive, they did not compare in any way with the beauty and elegance of Zivana.

Their faces were all covered with a white mask of cosmetic and in great contrast the translucence of Zivana's skin seemed to glow like a pearl as her name implied.

Their clothing was ornate and embroidered with pearls and jewels and heavy satins had been discarded for the gauzy apparel of summer.

Each concubine wore Manchu slippers with the raised heel embroidered and decorated in the most elaborate fashion.

The Prince's concubines were dressed in green, pink and orchid mauve, but Zivana for the first time that Stanton Ware had seen her was now wearing the palest daffodil-yellow embroidered with topazes and tiny diamonds.

There were the same stones shining in her dark hair and in the protectors of her long nails.

As she rose from her knees, her eyes downcast, her dark lashes on her pale cheeks, he wondered if it would be possible in the whole world to find a woman who was as beautiful.

The Prince's Number One concubine, Peach Blossom, started to entertain by singing a song which was a traditional favourite.

It was a love song, very sad and, Stanton Ware thought, somewhat dreary.

But he congratulated the singer warmly when she finished and she expressed her thanks by once again touching her forehead to the floor.

The second concubine had a more entertaining talent.

Small songbirds were brought into the room in a cage by one of the servants. She took them out one by one and made them perform by a series of soft whistles that told them what she required.

They ran up the sleeves of her gown to perch on her shoulders, they turned somersaults round an ivory stick that she held out for them and they opened their beaks and sang.

Then, at her command, they flew up to the ceiling to dive down again like small hawks, straight into their cage.

It was indeed an extremely clever performance and the Prince, who applauded the girls uproariously, looked gratified when both Li Hung-Chang and Stanton Ware told him how impressed they were by it.

The last of the Prince's concubines had a few magic tricks to show them with cards and little Chinese balls and coloured handkerchiefs, which she drew from the wide sleeves of her gown.

When she had finished her piece, the Prince looked at Zivana.

"The flowers I treasure have tried to entertain you, gentlemen," he said. "Can the lovely flower who is visiting us contribute to our enjoyment?"

Stanton Ware had no idea whether Zivana would accept or refuse such an invitation, but without hesitating she moved forward in the same manner as the other concubines had done.

She bowed with a grace that would have been impossible for any woman to equal let alone surpass, then, kneeling on the ground, she recited a poem.

It was a poem that had been written many centuries ago and it was a Chinese Classic, although Stanton Ware had never before heard it recited.

Like all Chinese poems, it used nature to symbolise the soul, the mind and the heart.

Because Zivana spoke it so movingly in her soft musical voice, he found himself carried away in his thoughts.

He felt that he might have been sitting at the feet of his Guru, who had taught him in a Lamasery the great truths hidden in the storehouses of knowledge amongst the snow-peaked mountains.

For a moment, because her voice was so compelling, Stanton Ware felt almost as if he left his body behind and journeyed free in time and space.

He knew in that passing second that the work he and Zivana had undertaken was but a pebble thrown into an ocean and yet the ripples of their actions might spread out, growing wider and ever wider towards an indefinite horizon.

Then, almost with a start, he came back to the reality of the present because Zivana had finished her poem and her voice was silent.

"Thank you, thank you, Perfect Pearl," he heard Prince Tuan say, "I have never heard that poem, or any other, so well rendered. It is as beautiful as you are yourself."

Zivana bowed low at his words and then he reached out his hand to help her to her feet, a gesture that might well have been a princely one, but Stanton Ware looked at him, a dawning suspicion in his eyes.

The Prince's ugly pockmarked face held an expression had made him draw in his breath sharply.

The concubines sat down and wine was brought for them, the Prince being boisterous and boastful, but Zivana was very quiet.

Stanton Ware really longed to know what she was thinking, but there was no chance of speaking to her privately. Only later when the concubines had withdrawn and Li Hung-Chang and Stanton Ware were saying 'goodnight' to the Prince did he say,

"So that you shall be comfortable in my house, Most Honourable Mandarin, and may I say how very honoured I am by your visit, I have put your concubine, Perfect Pearl, in the room next to yours."

"Your Highness is most thoughtful," Stanton Ware replied.

"Your servant is also near you," the Prince continued, "but, as he is very tired, as you also must be after such a long journey, one of my own men will sleep across your door so that, if you need anything, you have only to call."

Stanton Ware could only express his grateful thanks, but he knew that the servant would doubtless have long ears and anything he might say to Zivana would undoubtedly be repeated word for word back to the Prince.

He therefore retired to bed without making any effort to communicate with her in the next-door room.

But, as he lay in the darkness thinking of just how he should approach Li Hung-Chang, he could not help his thoughts returning to Zivana and recalling how lovely she had looked.

It was not only her beauty which had made the other concubines, attractive though they were, seem insignificant, it was also her breeding and she was comparable to a perfect piece of jade or a faultless pearl.

Stanton Ware felt as if her face was in front of his closed eyes.

He could see every feature, the curve of her lips, the strange lights in her eyes.

'She is truly named,' he thought.

Then he told himself that there was too much fire in her for a pearl to be the correct description.

Perhaps she was like an emerald, as green and unfathomable as a mountain pool or a ruby with the burning fires of the sun hidden in its depths.

He laughed because he was being ridiculously imaginative, but he was still thinking of her as he fell asleep.

*

The following morning, to Stanton Ware's relief, the Prince informed his guests after they had breakfasted that he had business to see to and he hoped that they would excuse him for an hour or so.

This was the opportunity that Stanton Ware had been waiting for.

No sooner had the Prince departed than he suggested to Li Hung-Chang that they should go into the garden.

To talk in the house or even in any of the many beautiful courtyards would have been to invite danger.

He had noted that among the Prince's entourage there were a great number of servants with keen intelligent faces, which told him that they were not merely servile creatures trained only to fetch and carry but had other attributes, which were undoubtedly of service to their Master.

The gardens were fragrant with the scent of flowers and nothing could be more beautiful, he thought, than spring in China.

They found a seat under a tree bowed down with pale pink blossoms, which against the blue of the sky was a subject worthy of any great artist.

"I have so longed for this opportunity to talk to you, Exalted Sir," Stanton Ware began frankly, "as Tseng-Wen said I could do."

"I had a feeling that was so," Li Hung-Chang replied.

"I came to Peking not out of curiosity nor because I was discontented with my very quiet uneventful life at home in the mountains," Stanton Ware went on, "but because I was deeply perturbed – "

"By what is happening in the country," Li Hung-Chang finished.

"You who have always been so progressively minded, you who pioneered China into the modern age, must also be worried and anxious as to where our country is being led at this particular time."

"It is true that I tried to bring progress to China," Li Hung-Chang answered, "but always I have had to fight desperately for everything I believed in."

"That I know, Noble Sir," Stanton Ware answered, "and yet you contrived to have the first railway built in your Province and the first telegraph wires."

"That is true, but the rest of China is a very different matter."

"Now the Boxers have pledged themselves to tear up the railways," Stanton Ware said, "and I believe that they will attack not only the Christians but, if they are opposed, our own people."

Li Hung-Chang nodded his head.

"I have seen for myself the Boxers roaming the streets," he said quietly, "and every day over a distance of several hundred miles they have not only set fire to many houses but have kidnapped people and even offered resistance to government troops."

"Surely the Dowager Empress knows this?" Stanton Ware asked.

"I am told that Her Majesty, surrounded by conflicting counsel, is refusing all demands to suppress the movement."

"Will she not listen to you?"

"That is why I am journeying to Peking," Li Hung-Chang answered. "But I am perturbed on hearing from you that there are Boxers so near to the Capital."

"If they have come so far North, there will be large numbers South of the City," Stanton Ware said.

He saw the old man's lips close into a hard line.

"I was told when I was last in Peking," he went on, "that the Ministers in the foreign Legations are not perturbed and that the killing of Christians is taken no more seriously than it has been in the past."

"The Legations will often see only what they wish to see," Li Hung-Chang said very enigmatically.

"It is what I have thought myself," Stanton Ware said, "but I learnt that each of the five Powers has troops which could be summoned to their defence if there was an emergency."

The old Viceroy did not flicker an eyelid and yet Stanton Ware was sure he had absorbed this information, storing it in his mind.

"Again I may be very wrong," he said tentatively, "but, having fought so fiercely to get a foothold in China, I cannot believe that the Great Powers will be driven away so easily."

"That is true," the Viceroy agreed. "What is more, the Imperial troops are not many in number."

"And how could it be possible for these dirty, untrained young Boxers to be of any use if it came to a war?"

"War is something that must not happen," Li Hung-Chang stipulated firmly.

"And yet as a country we seem to be drifting towards one," Stanton Ware insisted. "The Boxers are inflaming the ordinary people. One of their placards has already been displayed in a prominent place in the Chinese City."

"A placard from the Boxers? What did it say?"

Li Hung-Chang's question was sharp and betrayed far more effectively than anything he had said before that he was perturbed by the growing strength of the Boxer movement.

Stanton Ware recited the placard to him, remembering the words perfectly.

"The railways torn up," the Viceroy said almost beneath his breath.

He was obviously thinking of how proud he had been of the first railway, which he had been instrumental in building in his own Province.

Stanton Ware bent forward so that he could say in a very low voice,

"All the signs and portents, Exalted One, point to you as being the only man who can save China, the only man with the great history of your achievements behind you who could make the Dowager Empress listen to reason."

The Viceroy gave a deep sigh.

"Alas, I am no longer in Her Majesty's favour. She listens to those who encourage her to hate the foreigners and to believe that China is strong enough to fight alone."

"How could she hope to win?" Stanton Ware asked. "Surely someone is brave enough to tell her that the old prophecies all predict that this is a disastrous year, not a fortunate one, for China."

There was silence and then Stanton Ware said,

"Will you, Sir, be the saviour of a country you have worked and fought for all your life?"

"I will try," Li Hung-Chang said slowly, "I swear to you that I will try, but I am getting old now and who listens to an old man?"

There was a note of defeat in his voice, which struck Stanton Ware as being ominous.

Then he said,

"You are the only person amongst Her Majesty's advisors who not only loves China but also understands the West. You know what enormous ramifications the Great Powers have and you know how they will not be deflected from their purpose."

He paused to say impressively,

"Only you can make Her Majesty understand that compromise is the only course."

Li Hung-Chang seemed to straighten his shoulders as if he prepared himself for a battle ahead.

"I know where my duty lies," he said. "I shall strive to avert the hand of calamity and, if I cannot do so, then, when the fighting is over, I must negotiate the best possible terms from the conqueror whoever he may be."

Stanton Ware knew that the Viceroy was thinking aloud and he said,

"That is undoubtedly some consolation, Illustrious One, but I am hoping, because you are who you are, for a great deal more."

"You have much Diplomatic skill yourself, young man," Li Hung-Chang said as if he had thought of it for the first time. "Come with me to Peking and add your voice to mine."

"Alas, Sir, I carry little weight in the Forbidden City and I have been away from home for too long. But my thoughts and indeed my prayers will be with you for I really believe that at this particular hour in our history there is no one else we can turn to."

"You honour me," the Viceroy smiled.

Stanton Ware realised as they walked back in silence to The Palace that Li Hung-Chang was thinking deeply.

CHAPTER FOUR

As soon as Prince Tuan returned to The Palace, the Viceroy informed him that he was making arrangements to leave immediately for Peking.

Stanton Ware, watching the pockmarked face of the Prince, thought that the information annoyed him, but he knew it would be impossible to stop the old man from doing what he wished.

With what was obviously an effort, he accepted it with good grace.

As the Viceroy left the room to give instructions to his own servants, Stanton Ware said, bowing low,

"I must also be on my way, Your Highness. I have a long distance to travel and I have already trespassed for too long on your most generous hospitality."

"It has been a pleasure to have you," the Prince replied, "and I cannot allow you to leave with such precipitate haste. We have had so little time together to exchange all our interests."

Stanton Ware was about to insist that he must arrange for his departure when the Prince said,

"As soon as the Viceroy has left, there are a number of matters I should like to discuss with you privately as I have not been able to do in his presence."

This was too intriguing a proposition for Stanton Ware to refuse and he could only bow again and thank his host profusely.

He added, however, that he would stay the night, but must be on his way soon after dawn the following morning.

The Prince agreed to this and after a light repast they watched the Viceroy drive away from The Palace.

His entourage was certainly very impressive with the retainers in their colourful clothes riding horses behind his yellow carriage. The scene, Stanton Ware thought, would have made an extremely attractive subject for a dedicated painting.

The Viceroy's carriage, moving at a good pace with his attendants on horseback trotting behind it, was no sooner out of sight than Prince Tuan said to Stanton Ware,

"Let us sit in the garden. The sunshine is delightful after the cold of winter."

"I imagine that Your Highness spent the bleak months in Peking," Stanton Ware replied, knowing full well that the Prince had been in attendance upon the Empress.

He had in fact wondered why Prince Tuan had retired to his country Palace and he was now alert to learn everything he could from a man whom the more he saw of him the less he trusted him.

"The Viceroy, much as I have respect for him," the Prince began when they had seated themselves beside a large water-lily pool, "is from the old school. He believes that everything can be solved by democratic methods."

"Surely that is better than violence?" Stanton Ware ventured.

The Prince smiled unpleasantly.

"There are times," he said, "when only violence will achieve the effect one desires."

Stanton Ware did not reply.

He decided to say as little as possible, but to listen and remember every word.

"I know what your sentiments are, Honourable Mandarin," the Prince said, "but perhaps, living as you do among the mountains of Shantin, you do not understand the problems that beset Peking with the encroachment of the foreigners and their Legations taking up so much space in our Capital."

This, Stanton Ware thought to himself quickly, was exactly what he wanted to hear.

He stared at the flowers so that the Prince should not see the expression in his eyes and replied in a slow unintelligent voice,

"As Your Highness says, I have little knowledge of these problems."

"But they are extremely important to us," Prince Tuan retorted, "and so I am convinced that, as Her Majesty the Empress is beginning to realise, until we get rid of the foreign devils China will never be a strong country."

This, Stanton Ware thought, was coming straight out into the open and, after a moment's pause, he said with a well-simulated note of ignorance in his voice,

"Surely, Sir, it is important for us as a nation to trade?"

"We can easily be self-sufficient," Prince Tuan replied almost angrily. "What good will railways and telegraphs do ruining our lovely landscape and encouraging restlessness among the peasants?"

This was the real reason for his strong objections to progress, Stanton Ware thought, the peasants might no longer be willing to act as slaves to their overlords.

Modernisation might make them resent the fact that they had to work intolerably hard to pay their exorbitant taxes.

There was silence and after a moment Stanton Ware said tentatively,

"The foreign devils are firmly ensconced. How can we ever be rid of them?"

He looked at the Prince as he spoke and saw a sudden gleam in his small eyes.

He felt that he was about to receive a truthful answer, but the Prince must have thought better about over-confiding in him for he said,

"There will doubtless be ways and means by which this can be accomplished."

Stanton Ware looked puzzled.

"You are very much wiser than I am, Your Highness, but I find it difficult to conceive how they can be driven out unless we have a mighty Army!"

The Prince did not reply and Stanton Ware went on,

"From what I have learnt in Peking, the Imperial troops find it quite hard enough as it is to keep order over the whole country."

"That is true," Prince Tuan agreed, "but I have ideas concerning this matter."

He forced a smile to his narrow lips as he said,

"I would like to think that I could count on your support at the Conference that will take place shortly in the Council Chamber in the Forbidden City."

"I should be honoured to be of any assistance," Stanton Ware replied humbly.

"That is good," the Prince said. "And if necessary I will send a messenger to your home in Shantin to ask you to come to Peking with all possible speed."

Stanton Ware bowed his acceptance.

As the Prince then talked of other matters, he told himself that he had not learnt much except that the Prince had some ideas up his sleeve which undoubtedly spelt danger to the Legations.

The rest of the day passed slowly.

Stanton Ware instructed Yin that they would leave early in the morning and the luggage was packed except for the Mandarin's coat that he would change into for dinner.

It was an extremely magnificent coat that Tseng-Wen had provided for him, embroidered with seed pearls and coral and the eight Felicitons Buddhist emblems.

To his surprise, after they had dined alone, the Prince did not suggest that they should be joined by the concubines.

Stanton Ware was extremely relieved.

He had seen the way that Prince Tuan had looked at Perfect Pearl the night before and, whenever he thought about it, he told himself that the sooner they were well away from The Palace the better.

When dinner was over and they were seated on silken-cushioned couches, Prince Tuan said,

"I would not like to think I was remiss in any hospitality I might offer you, Most Noble Mandarin."

"Your hospitality has been overwhelmingly gracious," Stanton Ware replied.

There was a little pause.

Then the Prince said,

"Today a new flower was brought to my Palace, young, untouched, pure and of a great beauty, from the other side of the Great Wall near Jehol."

"Your Highness is fortunate," Stanton Ware said, "the Manchurian women of those parts are famous for their beauty."

"I am glad you have heard of them," the Prince remarked, "for I would like to make you a gift of this exquisite creature, whose name is 'White Magnolia'."

Stanton Ware stiffened as he realised suddenly the whole import of what the Prince was saying.

"I feel sure you will agree with me," Prince Tuan went on before he could speak, "that a man who is adventurous will always wish to taste a different fruit from what he has enjoyed before."

Stanton Ware forced a smile to his lips.

"You are very gracious, Your Highness, but if one is content by a warm fire, why seek another?"

He saw an expression of anger flash across the Prince's face because he had not accepted his gift immediately, but suavely, lying back apparently at his ease, he replied,

"The Taoist sage, Peng-Isu, said that to derive the greatest benefit from sexual enjoyment a man should make love to virgins, which will restore his youthful looks."

Stanton Ware laughed and it was a sound of genuine amusement.

"That is good advice for those who are growing too old like the Viceroy, but for us, Your Highness, praise to the Gods, there are many years of virility left."

He gave the Prince only a fleeting glance, but there was no mistaking the frown between the brows and the surly expression on his face.

"Some men prefer great experience," he said after several seconds had ticked by. "My concubine, Peach

Blossom, is greatly enamoured of you. I cannot believe that you would not wish to make her happy before you leave."

"My concubine, Perfect Pearl, is of a jealous nature," Stanton Ware replied. "I would not hurt her."

They were no longer fencing, he thought, but were speaking openly and he knew that the Prince was determined to bargain with him for Zivana and he braced himself for the combat.

"Doubtless Perfect Pearl would be consoled with jewels or a change of environment," the Prince suggested.

Stanton Ware straightened himself.

"I very much think, Most Honoured Host," he said coldly, "that we waste precious time in concerning ourselves with the vagaries of women."

There was no mistaking the anger in Prince Tuan's face as he realised that Stanton Ware had slammed shut the door of negotiations.

Before the Prince could speak, Stanton Ware went on,

"Would men of intelligence, such as ourselves, Your Highness, when they feel tremors of an earthquake, stop to pick a flower?"

The Prince did not answer and he continued,

"Tomorrow morning Perfect Pearl and I will leave your Palace before Your Highness has been awakened. Would you permit me now to retire and then to thank you with the utmost sincerity for your most gracious and lavish hospitality?"

Stanton Ware rose and bowed.

Because he was so disgruntled and so angry at being refused what he desired, the Prince made no effort to rise as courtesy decreed.

He merely lay back against his cushions, looking surly and biting one of his fingernails.

Slowly and without appearing to be in any haste, Stanton Ware withdrew from the room, then went upstairs to his bedroom, where Yin was waiting for him.

There was no question of having any private conversation for the Prince's servants who were outside in the corridor could undoubtedly overhear everything that was spoken.

As usual in China, the walls of the room were not substantial, but delicate wood painted in glorious colours depicting landscapes, phoenixes, storks, and dragons.

They had, however, a fragility that made it only too easy for anyone outside the room to hear what was being done or said should they wish to do so.

The *K'ang*, or bed, on which Stanton Ware had slept the night before was ten feet long and made of bricks under which a fire was lit in the winter to keep the sleeper warm.

It had hangings of crêpe and red satin woven with a design of birds and lucky symbols.

The pillows were filled with down, like the coverlet, while others contained herbs whose fragrance scented the whole room.

The doors, as was usual, did not open or close in the Western manner, but slid along the walls.

In Stanton Ware's room there was one door that opened onto the passage and another one that communicated with the next bedroom where Zivana slept.

He asked Yin in sign language if she was in her room and the servant understood and nodded.

"We leave as soon as it is dawn," Stanton Ware said aloud.

"Everything is ready, Noble Master," Yin replied.

As Stanton Ware was ready for bed, Yin went from the room, bowing low as he stepped into the passage and slid the door closed behind him.

Stanton Ware climbed onto the *K'ang* and lay back on the pillows, thinking with relief that their visit had come to an end and tomorrow he could leave.

He was not certain if he had achieved anything except that the Viceroy had left for Peking and he could only hope that if he saw the Boxers on the way he would be as perturbed by their presence as he and Zivana had been.

*

In her room Zivana had heard Stanton Ware come to bed and she felt an inexpressible relief as she had the night before that he was near her.

She had known ever since she came to The Palace that it had an evil atmosphere which emanated from its owner.

From the very moment she had set eyes on Prince Tuan's pock-marked face and seen his expression when he looked at her she had been afraid.

She had known that he was wicked, in fact she had learnt quite a lot about him and his behaviour before she arrived in his Palace.

When she had been in touch with her friends in the Forbidden City, she had learned from them that Prince Tuan was trying very hard to gain ascendancy over the Dowager Empress.

As a young girl Tz'u-hsi had flung herself into the pleasures of Palace life and favoured masculine aggressive men who were a vivid contrast to the effeminacy of the eunuchs. It had been rumoured for years that she had taken as her lover, Jung-lu, who was one of China's most outstanding Generals and a very strong personality.

Although politically he was unimaginative and most often undecided as the Empress's favourite, he rose to the highest positions in the land.

But in 1878, Jung-lu, a virile soldier of forty-three, had fallen from grace.

The Empress was just a year older than he was, but for a woman that was considered old.

It was whispered amongst those in the know that Jung-lu had been caught red-handed with a lady of The Palace and that the Empress had acted like a woman scorned and there was no holding her.

Jung-lu had not been recalled to office for more than six years but by then Tz'u-hsi had created for herself the image of an old and venerated Dowager, too staid and too fastidious for voluptuous dalliance.

It was impossible for Jung-lu, even though he was necessary to the affairs of China, to be completely reinstated in the Dowager's affections and this was where Prince Tuan had come in.

He was ugly and unprepossessing to look at, but he had a boisterous, rowdy overbearing manner that pleased the old Empress, who at sixty-five still liked a man to be a man.

But Zivana had known the moment she first saw him that he was evil and she was quite certain that he was planning something that was disastrously wicked.

The favourite among his concubines was undoubtedly Peach Blossom, who had been with him for some years.

She was most intelligent, Zivana felt, and she felt certain that, if Peach Blossom knew anything of her Master's plans, she could somehow be coaxed into revealing them.

The fact that they were not asked to entertain the gentlemen as they had the night before gave Zivana the opportunity she needed to talk to Peach Blossom alone.

It was easy enough to make her boast of her Master's prowess not only as a lover but as a Statesman and a powerful influence in China.

Zivana was clever and by the time she retired to her bed she had found out all that she wished to know.

Like Stanton Ware, she knew that everything that was said in their bedrooms would be overheard by the servants sleeping outside their doors.

It was quite unnecessary that she should be guarded as well as Stanton Ware. She was sure, therefore, that the guard was there not because the Prince was concerned either for their safety or their comfort but because he wished to spy on them and have reported to him what they said when they were alone together.

Last night, since they did not communicate in any way, he must have been disappointed, but Zivana had not missed the way that he had looked at her.

What Stanton Ware did not know was that the Prince had come to the women's quarters that evening ostensibly to talk to his own concubines.

They had greeted him with cries of pleasure and, when they had made their obeisance, in which Zivana also joined, he had talked to her.

As he did so, his eyes flickered over her face and her body so that she felt that mentally he stripped her naked.

"My little lovebirds are looking after you, I hope?" he asked. "You have everything you want?"

"Everything, Your Highness."

"Your Master is lucky. Where can he have found a pearl of such beauty?"

"I had the privilege of meeting such a very wonderful man as my Master at the house of Tseng-Wen," Zivana replied truthfully.

"I know Tseng-Wen," the Prince said. "When he was finding you a protector I wish that he had thought of me."

Zivana bowed her head but did not speak.

"It is a pity – a great pity," the Prince said.

There was something in the tone of his voice and the look in his eyes that made Zivana feel afraid.

She had, however, forced her fears away and then made herself concentrate on Peach Blossom.

But now even in her own room with Stanton Ware next door she had an uncomfortable feeling that Prince Tuan was reaching out to her.

Because of the work she had been doing in Peking and because all her life she had been trained to be perceptive and ultra-sensitive, every nerve of her body was alerted to danger.

She walked towards her *K'ang* where it stood in an alcove.

It was smaller and not as impressive as Stanton Ware's, but it was comfortable and hung with pale pink satin curtains embroidered with flowers.

Zivana knew that she would not rest in it and she wondered if she could go into Stanton Ware's room and tell him how perturbed she felt.

But suppose he misunderstood her reasons for approaching him and did not realise that she was motivated entirely by a concern for their work together?

Then she told herself that she was being absurd,

He had never shown in any way that he was interested in her as a woman.

It might be English self-control, but she wondered if perhaps he was too dedicated to his career to have any interests outside it.

Then she remembered that he had met Tseng-Wen through the instigation of Diverse Delight.

Tseng-Wen had told her quite frankly what Diverse Delight's position was in Peking and how the 'House of a Thousand Joys' was of considerable importance to those who looked for information from the Ministers who went there in search of entertainment.

Zivana had accepted what she had been told without being curious or interested.

But now, remembering how warmly Tseng-Wen had spoken about Diverse Delight, she found herself wondering what she had meant to Stanton Ware.

Almost for the first time since she had known him she realised how attractive he was as a man.

At first she had been too busy hating him to think of him as anything but an insufferable Englishman, a stiff-necked and arrogant example of those who had hurt and distressed her mother.

Then, when they had talked together, she realised how clever he was and in many ways as perceptive as she was herself and her feelings had gradually begun to change.

She found herself thinking of him as a friend whom she could trust and who she could work with.

Now she saw that he was a man and attractive in a way that Prince Tuan could never be.

She had only to think of the Prince to shiver and because her mouth suddenly felt dry she moved across the room to where there was a pitcher of water on a table that stood against the wall of the corridor.

Zivana had blown out the candles, but there was a faint light from a piece of transparent alabaster that stood over the lintel of the door.

The alabaster was engraved with the charm of 'good luck' and was so fine and so perfect that through the faintly veined stone came enough light for her to find her way and to pour some water into a glass.

She had just raised it to her lips when she heard the very faint sound of footsteps in the passage outside.

They were so faint that she would not have heard them had she been lying in her bed in the alcove.

They were the footsteps of two men, she decided. Then she heard the servant who lay across her door raise himself.

Without thinking about what she was doing, she moved a little nearer and placing her ear against the painted wood she heard the man say, hardly breathing the words,

"What do you want?"

The answer was so faint that it was no more than the drawing of a breath and yet Zivana heard it.

"The woman is to be taken to the Prince!"

She heard the sound of the servant moving away from the door, then swiftly, so swiftly that it was like a bird in flight, Zivana sped across the room.

She slipped back the door that communicated with Stanton Ware's bedroom.

She entered and closed it behind her, knowing even as she did so that the door from the passage into her room opened silently.

*

Stanton Ware had almost fallen asleep.

He had been going over in his mind what had been said during the day and he had come, as if in full circle, to his conversation with the Prince after dinner.

His first reaction was to believe it an intolerable suggestion that he should hand over his own concubine, whether it was Zivana or anyone else.

He felt that the Prince was abusing his position as a host to suggest such an exchange.

But he was honest enough with himself to know that such things often happened.

There was nothing odd in the Prince's suggestion, as he had already paid lip service to the rules of hospitality by offering his guest another concubine.

That no girl, virgin or otherwise, could have been an equal exchange for Zivana was a point that did not arise.

What mattered, Stanton Ware knew, was that the Prince had been rebuffed and he had an uncomfortable feeling that the matter would not rest there.

'The sooner we are away from here the better!' he told himself firmly.

He found his eyes closing as if the sooner he slept the quicker tomorrow would come.

Then he heard a slight sound, but he did not realise it was the communicating door of his bedroom opening, although it brought him to wakefulness as a man awakes who is used to danger.

In a split second he was tense and ready for anything that might happen.

Then from the foot of the bed he heard a soft voice say,

"Most Noble and Exalted Lord, your humble concubine, Perfect Pearl, asks permission to approach you in humility and in submission to your will."

For a moment he was astonished that Zivana was there and then he understood.

She had a reason for coming and was in the process of warning him that what she was saying was overheard.

It was essential that those who were listening should believe that she was just performing the function she had been brought on the journey for.

As her voice died away, Stanton Ware replied,

"Approach, Perfect Pearl. I welcome you and I was in fact waiting impatiently for you to come to me. Without you close beside me the night would be long and dark."

He knew she moved a little nearer to him from the foot of the bed and he went on,

"I need your warmth, I need your softness and my head aches like my heart does from the worry and perplexity of these last few days."

"I will make you forget your troubles, Most Exalted One, who is more handsome than all the heroes of our history and is in truth as one of the Gods themselves."

"Careful, child, in case you make them jealous!" Stanton Ware smiled.

"Can the Gods be jealous of their own?" Perfect Pearl asked.

She had moved up the bed towards him and now she laid her head down on the pillow beside him.

He did not touch her, but, because he knew that it would be expected by the listeners, he said and his voice was deep,

"Your hair is like silk and your skin as the petal of the rose. Many women are beautiful, but you are more beautiful than any flower I have ever seen!"

"Your words make me shy," Zivana answered. "Never was a man so strong and yet your hands can be so gentle and your lips can lift me high above the peaks of the snow-capped mountains."

Her voice was low and yet just loud enough for those who would be listening outside the room to hear what was being said.

Then so softly that her mouth almost touched his ear she whispered,

"Two men came to my room to – take me to the – Prince."

Stanton Ware stiffened with anger.

Aloud he said,

"Last night we were tired, but tonight you will stay with me until dawn breaks. I missed the fragrance of your hair and the sweetness of your breath."

As he spoke, acting the part that was required of him, he was aware that Zivana smelt of lilies.

Most concubines used the heavy Eastern perfumes of musk or sandalwood, which he had always disliked.

The fragrance that came from Zivana was very faint and yet it had a sweetness and purity about it, which made him think of her profile silhouetted against the lilies in Tseng-Wen's courtyard.

As they lay there close against each other and yet not touching, Stanton Ware suddenly found his heart beating tumultuously.

An almost uncontrollable impulse swept over him to hold Zivana close against him, to kiss her and to feel in actual fact, as he was pretending to do, her softness and her warmth.

He felt his desire for her rise in his body like a tidal wave, sweeping away pretence, restraint, even thought, through its sheer force.

It was agony not to give way to the impulse that throbbed within him, making the sweat burst out on his forehead, his mouth feel dry and his voice constricted in his throat.

'I want her! *Oh, God, I want her*! he thought.

Then he knew that this was only the culmination of what he had been feeling since the first moment he had seen her.

She was so exquisite and lovely that any man would have been swept off his feet by her looks alone.

But when he had talked to Zivana, when he realised her intelligence and the depth of her thinking, love had been born in him to grow and deepen day by day.

Because he knew that, while Zivana was trying to give him her friendship, she had no other feelings for him and he had forced himself not to think of her in any way except as a companion.

Only when he had seen Prince Tuan's evil eyes lusting after her last night had he known a sudden surge of furious rage and jealousy.

It had swept through him uncontrollably and made him long to put his hands round the Prince's throat and throttle him.

To think now that the Prince was prepared to abuse the laws of hospitality and to take by force what had been refused made Stanton Ware ready to do murder.

But he knew it would serve no useful purpose to make a scene.

They were to all intents and purposes alone in the camp of the enemy and so there was nothing he could do for the moment but play for safety and keep Zivana beside him.

It was unlikely that the Prince would dare to send his men into his bedroom.

But it would have been possible to spirit Zivana away without him being aware of it had she not come to him for protection.

The Prince's men would doubtless be very adept, as all Chinese were, at moving into a room so silently that Zivana would have been gagged and helpless before she even realised that they were there.

She would have been taken to the Prince's apartments and after that there would have been no escape!

Perhaps in the morning she would have been given back to Stanton Ware, perhaps not. Either way there would have been nothing he could do about it.

Concubines were of little importance and, even if she vanished completely, it would have been hard to know who he could appeal to for assistance in finding her again.

As the terror of what might have happened came to his mind, he wanted to pull Zivana into his arms, kiss her a thousand times and assure her that he would fight for her until his dying breath.

Instead he lay stiffly beside her and after a moment she whispered,

"I have something of – importance to tell you – "

"What is it?" he asked.

"Peach Blossom tells me that the Boxers are coming from every part of the country to congregate around Peking and will enter the City at a given signal."

"Who will give the signal?"

"The Prince!"

"When?"

"On the thirteenth of the month."

He knew at once that this was news of the utmost urgency.

Li Hung-Chang must be told immediately, he thought, and so must Herbert Squiers.

"Peach Blossom is sure of this?"

Zivana did not answer, but he knew that she nodded her head.

"We must get back to Peking," he said. "We will start off by travelling North as if we are going to Shantin and then make a detour."

He knew that she understood.

Then, remembering those who were listening, he said in a louder tone,

"You are so perfect! The joy you give me, Perfect Pearl, is greater than any I have ever known before."

"All I want is to make you happy," Zivana answered.

"You have made me happy," Stanton Ware replied, "but now we must sleep for we have a long journey before us tomorrow and I would not have you exhausted."

Because it was impossible to speak to her without his voice deepening with the intensity of his emotions, Stanton Ware knew that he sounded very convincing.

It was agony to feel Zivana so near to him, yet to know that he must not touch her and that, if he did so, she might be frightened.

He turned over so that his back was towards her.

"Sleep," he said, trying to sound as if he yawned. "I am tired, but you are close to me and that gives me a deep content."

"The Gods bring you sweet dreams," Zivana replied. "You are a man above men, a lover of whom any woman would be proud."

'This may be play-acting,' Stanton Ware thought, 'but I wish to God it was the truth!'

He felt his body throbbing and his heart beating so violently that it almost seemed to leap from his breast.

He lay on his side with his back towards her and he heard her settle herself with her head on one of the pillows and pull the silken coverlet filled with down close around her body.

They were safe on the *K'ang* but he realised that he would not sleep, not only because he wished to keep watch on Zivana but because the fires burning within him made it impossible for him to relax.

He wanted her, he desired her, he longed for her as he told himself he had never longed for a woman before.

'One day I will make her love me,' he vowed silently.

*

They set off the following morning and, as Stanton Ware had expected, the Prince was not there to see them go.

His Comptroller, his Secretary, his Groom of the Chambers and a dozen senior servants saw them off with invocations to the Gods to protect them and bring them good fortune.

Finally the carriage carried Stanton Ware and Zivana away out through the garden and into the Park beyond.

His servants had their explicit instructions from Yin and, when they reached the gates, they turned North instead of taking the road to Peking.

This meant that they travelled along the foot of the Western Mountains and the rising sun touched the tall silver pines that were unique in the Peking Valley.

They had been extolled in thousands of poems, which even so could not find the right words for such beauty.

They had driven for maybe a quarter of a mile when to Stanton Ware's surprise Yin drew the carriage to a standstill and opened the door to say,

"Forgive me, Master, but I forgot to hand you the book of meditation that you told me you wished to read during the journey. It was most remiss of me and I must humbly beg your indulgence."

He put a small leather-covered book into Stanton Ware's hands as he spoke.

Realising that this was an excuse and there was another reason for the hold-up, Stanton Ware replied,

"Thank you, Yin, I was just about to ask you for this manual."

Yin bent forward to tuck the rug a little closer round Stanton Ware's legs, then said in a whisper,

"In half an hour's time, Sir, demand that we stop so that you can have a drink."

He moved out of the carriage as he spoke and Stanton Ware said loudly,

"My meditations are disturbed by these early morning departures. I shall be glad when I am home and life returns to normal."

Before he finished speaking Yin had resumed his seat on the box of the carriage and they were moving off once more.

Zivana had heard what he said and she asked in a low voice, .

"What do you think is wrong?"

"I have no idea," Stanton Ware answered.

Now that the carriage was moving again, if they talked in low voices it was impossible for the servants riding on either side of it to hear what was being said.

"You do not think the Prince will have us followed?" Zivana asked after a moment.

"I think it unlikely," Stanton Ware replied. "At the same time we must travel for at least two hours in this direction before I produce some excuse for returning to Peking."

"I think that a presentiment would be a good idea," she suggested with a little smile, "a presentiment of illness for your friend, Tseng-Wen, which has come to you in a vision."

"Do you think these men would believe that?" Stanton Ware asked in an amused voice.

"They will want to believe it. Signs, portents and omens are not just efficacious, but I am certain that they would rather stay in Peking than travel to the mountains of Shantin."

Stanton Ware laughed.

"You are right there. I thought that there was no pleasure on their faces as we left this morning even though they know that they will be well paid for the journey."

"Mark my words," Zivana said, "as soon as they turn their faces towards the City they will be straining like horses returning to their stables to get there as quickly as possible."

"I am sure you are right," Stanton Ware agreed, "and that will suit me. I want to give your information to Li Hung-Chang to strengthen his hand when he is trying to convince the Dowager Empress what a danger the Boxers can be."

"The Old Buddha believes what she wants to believe and nothing that she does not."

"Then she will not have to wait long before she learns the truth."

Zivana sighed.

"How can she and the Council be so stupid? Surely they realise that all the might of the Boxers will not drive the Great Powers away forever?"

"The Prince is an evil unscrupulous man," Stanton Ware said. "I do not believe he cares a hoot about China but only for himself."

As he spoke vehemently, he knew it was impossible for him to judge the Prince fairly or consider him without heat.

All night, as he and Zivana had lain back-to-back on the big *K'ang*, he had found himself seething with anger at the Prince's horrible scheme to take her as a captive to his apartments.

Even to think of Zivana in proximity to that pockmarked evil man made Stanton Ware clench and reclench his hands with the force of his feelings.

'If I ever kill anybody in cold blood,' he told himself, 'it will be Prince Tuan and the world will be a cleaner place without him.'

But his own Palace, filled with an enormous company of servants, was certainly not the place for murder.

Equally he was thankful that he did not have to look on the Prince's hideous face before they left or to see his ferret-like eyes dwelling on Zivana's exquisite beauty.

It had been a crazy scheme, he felt, to allow her to act the part of a concubine. Yet at the same time what Tseng-Wen had visualised her doing had proved to be remarkably accurate.

Without Zivana, even though he guessed at the Prince's involvement with the Boxers, he would never have known the actual date that they planned to storm the Capital.

The difficulty, he knew, would be to convince anyone of what was going to happen or to make them realise that they must take steps to prevent it.

He had not forgotten the pig-headed obtuseness of the British Minister or the fact that his American counterpart was equally blind and complacent.

"We must hurry to Peking," Stanton Ware said aloud.

Zivana flashed a smile at him and he knew that she understood what he was feeling.

"It is annoying to think that there must be any delay," he went on, "but we had better do as Yin wants."

He shouted to the coachman to stop and then he said,

"I want a drink. The wine I consumed last night has left my mouth as dry as the desert. We will rest here for a few minutes in the shade of a tree."

"As the sun is already growing hot, Master," Yin replied, "have I permission to take the carriage a little way off the road. Later the horses will travel swifter if they are away from the flies."

"Do as you please," Stanton Ware replied in a disagreeable voice.

As he spoke, he saw two of the outriders glance at each other as if they were amused at having such an irascible Master.

Yin had the carriage turned up a track that wound amongst some trees.

When they were out of sight of the road, Yin told the coachman to come to a standstill and the servants who had been riding dismounted.

The horses, swishing their tails, started to crop the grass.

"If, Most Noble Master, you would walk a little way higher," Yin said, "there is a place where you would be comfortable. I will bring wine for yourself and for the lady and I am sure that the headache which has plagued you all night will soon be better."

"I hope so," Stanton Ware said in gloomy tones as if he thought it unlikely.

He and Zivana walked away from the carriage over the mossy ground between the silver pines and, as soon as they were out of earshot, Yin was beside them.

"Quickly, Master!" he said urgently. "There is no time to be lost. The Prince has given orders that his servants are to overtake you."

"His servants!" Zivana exclaimed with a little cry.

"I overheard what was said before we left The Palace," Yin explained, "but there were no chances to inform you of the plan."

"What does the Prince intend to do with us?" Stanton Ware asked.

"You, Master, will have a most regrettable accident. And you will die and the lady will be taken back to The Palace."

"What shall we do?"

"I have brought along with me two coolie outfits for you," Yin said. "If you will divest yourselves of what you are wearing, I will fetch the wine from the carriage."

He set down what appeared to be two cushions at their feet, but then the silk covers were unstitched and Zivana drew from one a coolie *custer* or a large straw hat

Then with a glance at Stanton Ware she hurried behind a pine tree and started to take off her elaborate pink satin coat and her pearl-studded Manchu shoes and draw the jewelled pins from her dark hair.

A few minutes later Stanton Ware, wearing the blue coolie tunic and trousers that were the standard dress for both Chinese men and women, saw Zivana come from behind the tree.

She was dressed exactly as he was except for the fact that her figure was so slender that she might have been a boy.

They wore the usual clumsy flat sandals held together by a leather thong between the first and second toe.

Zivana had bound her head with a handkerchief that almost completely hid her dark hair and she placed over it the wide-brimmed rough straw hat that protected all those who worked in the fields from the heat of the sun.

Yin collected their discarded garments, slipping Zivana's pins and nail protectors into his pocket.

"Follow me, Honourable Sir," he said to Stanton Ware.

He went ahead of them up a twisting path that climbed between the pines until just ahead they saw the mountain begin to rise steeply.

Here there were craggy rocks where there were a number of open caves.

Stanton Ware looked at them and Yin said,

"You will find, Sir, that there are caves in these mountains right up to the summit. Go as far as you can and if you hear the Prince's men you must find one where you can hide."

"That is what we will do," Stanton Ware agreed, "and you – ?"

"As soon as possible I will return to Peking and warn my Master of what has occurred."

"Tell him to inform Li Hung-Chang at once that the Boxers are converging on Peking and will enter the City on the thirteenth of June, led by Prince Tuan."

Yin nodded.

"I thought that is what would happen, Sir," he said, "but I did not know the date."

"Also inform Mr. Herbert Squiers of the American Legation. Tell him you come from me. He will be expecting a communication."

"That I will do," Yin promised, "but now, Noble Sir, you must hurry!"

He gave them a bag that contained food and then, carrying their discarded clothes a little further, he stuffed them deep down into a hole that would be too small for men searching for human beings to investigate.

He pushed them in so far that just the soles of his feet could be seen, then as he emerged, brushing the sand from his clothes, Stanton Ware asked,

"You have money?"

"Plenty, sir, and you will need what you have with you."

Yin, who had dressed and undressed Stanton Ware, was well aware that he wore a belt round his waist with a large amount of Chinese money in it.

"Hurry, Noble Sir," Yin said urgently. "I will return slowly to the carriage and tell the servants because you drank so much last night you are now asleep."

"Thank you, Yin, and take care of yourself," Stanton Ware said.

He put out his hand and took Zivana's.

"We have a stiff climb ahead of us," he said in a calm voice.

They set off together without looking back.

CHAPTER FIVE

"Are your feet sore?" Stanton Ware asked.

Zivana flashed him a smile.

"I have walked in more comfortable shoes."

"I have walked for so many miles in these sorts of sandals," he said, "that my feet have grown used to them. But I have been worrying about yours."

"There are worse things to worry about," Zivana replied.

That was true, Stanton Ware knew. At the same time, sitting on the mossy rocks with a narrow river running crystal clear below them, it was hard to remember that they were still very much in danger.

They had climbed higher and higher until, although they were still among the pine trees, they were not far from the summit of one of the mountains.

It had grown hotter and very airless beneath the branches of the tall silver pines and he was thinking of Zivana when he suggested that they sit down and eat some of the food that Yin had given them.

She had not complained, although he knew that the climb would have been strenuous for a man let alone a woman. The leather thong between her toes must be agony as it rubbed raw the softness of her skin.

They ate some of the food, which, because it had come from The Palace, was both exotic and delicious.

Although Stanton Ware said nothing, he thought that it would be some time before they enjoyed such a meal again.

He was relieved to see that in the bag that Yin had handed him was a razor, which he would require both for his chin and for his head, together with a bottle of the gum that was used on their eyes.

"What do you intend to do now?" Zivana asked him.

"I think we must walk South along the top of the mountain since the Prince's men will expect us to go North."

She nodded her head and then, looking down at the tumbling water below them, she said,

"It will be cold tonight. I am sure that this river comes from the snow on the peaks."

"We will find somewhere sheltered," Stanton Ware answered confidently.

But, although he did not intend Zivana to know it, he was feeling anxious.

He knew better than she did what it was like to be exposed on a mountainside when the snows were still thick on the summit and the wind whistled through the trees.

He picked up what food they had left and put it back into the bag, being careful as he did so to leave no trace of where they had been sitting.

Then, before he could rise to his feet, far away in the distance he heard voices.

He looked at Zivana and knew that she had heard them too. Without speaking they both sprang to their feet and started to climb once again the rocky crags which were so exhausting.

Perhaps they were tired, or perhaps he was over-anxious, but it seemed to Stanton Ware that it was even more difficult than it had been before to climb and to go on climbing.

Now they would pull themselves up onto great rocks, only to find other even larger ones ahead of them.

At another time he would have noticed that they were moving through a very strange and exotically beautiful landscape.

The huge trunks of the pines were like pillars of beaten silver and their branches beneath the new green shoots of the spring were as black as night.

It seemed to grow utterly silent now that the river that had thundered beneath them was far away and there was in fact a weird solemnity that was hard to explain.

Still in the far distance, but, as Stanton Ware thought, coming nearer, were the sounds of men's voices calling to one another.

He thought that he could hear the noise of sticks beating the undergrowth almost as if they wished to flush out a wild animal

' 'That is what we are,' he told himself, 'animals to be hunted down and destroyed – '

They had been climbing for over two hours and feeling that it was going to be difficult to escape from their pursuers, when he began to look for a cave that they could hide in as Yin had suggested. But here, so high up in the mountain, the caves were hard to find.

Then, as he was searching between the trees, he saw a Temple.

For a moment he felt almost as if it was a mirage, then he realised that it was in fact an ancient Temple, very probably deserted.

As they drew nearer, they could see that it was approached by a long flight of steps that led into a courtyard and then there were more steps leading into the Temple itself.

Round the courtyard grew ancient pines like silver pillars.

Stanton Ware realised that beyond the first Temple there were other courtyards and other buildings, each one separated from the next.

He thought that once there must have been many Monks dwelling and worshipping here, but now he saw that the weeds were lifting the stones of the courtyard and so he was sure that when they reached the Temple it would be empty and desolate and there would be only bats hanging from its carved beams.

At the same time he thought it might afford a hiding place and, as they reached the steps he and Zivana ran up them and there was no need to explain to her the danger they were in.

They crossed over the courtyard, their sandals flapping on the stones and then, climbing the second flight of steps, they saw that the Temple was larger than they had expected.

It had an upward-sweeping tile roof and the usual horned projections at the four corners to repel evil influences.

The doors, once painted in bright colours but now faded and cracked, were open and they went inside.

There was a huge cavernous hall, which seemed for the moment almost completely dark until, as their eyes grew used to it, they could see a colossal golden figure of Buddha seated in the lotus position.

With his huge hands clasped in timeless calm, he seemed just like a supernatural image floating on a sea of their imagination.

Then Stanton Ware saw that right in front of the statue there was a brass bowl and in it a number of incense sticks while the fragrance and smoke from them rose up in blue spirals.

As he and Zivana stood there surprised and somewhat uncertain of what to do next, they heard, coming from the shadows, footsteps moving with the softness of someone who walks without shoes.

Before he saw him Stanton Ware knew that he was a Priest and, as he walked forward, he was looking with searching eyes at the man's face.

There were two types of Buddhist Priests in China then, the stupid placid men who come from the people and the old aristocratic race of scholars with high distinguished faces.

As he peered in the darkness of the Temple to see which sort this Priest was, Stanton Ware was praying that here they would find the help they needed.

The Priest reached them and they saw that he was a man who had dignity and also a look of spirituality about him

His robe, of poor material, was clean and cared for and, although he looked at Stanton Ware and Zivana with the cold enigmatic stare of the Chinese, there was a keenness about his eyes.

Stanton Ware bowed low and said,

"We seek sanctuary, Your Holiness."

The Priest's eyes did not change, his face was like a mask.

"I ask it in the name of the Jewel in the Lotus," Stanton Ware continued.

As he spoke, he made the secret sign known only to those who have studied in the great Lamasery where Lamas have a Freemasonry of their own, which is secret from the rest of the world.

For a moment the Priest stared at Stanton Ware incredulously.

Then before he could speak there was behind them the sound of men breaking their way through the brushwood below the pines and their voices echoing upwards seeming to vibrate across the empty courtyard.

"Help us," Stanton Ware begged desperately.

The Priest turned and said one word,

"Come!"

They followed him into the shadows that he had emerged from and, because it was so dark, Stanton Ware reached out to take Zivana's hand in his.

Linked together, yet totally unable to walk side by side because of the narrowness of the passage they were being led through, they moved along until suddenly Stanton Ware realised that they were behind the great statue of the Buddha.

The Priest stopped, and he must have touched a secret spring, for there before them was a narrow aperture in the gold of the Lotus that the God was sitting on.

With a gesture of his hand he beckoned them into it.

They had to bend almost double to enter, but, when they were inside, the space was as high as the figure of the Buddha himself.

Stanton Ware heard the faintest click as the door shut behind them and at the same time he heard the footsteps of their pursuers ringing out on the stone steps.

They were shouting at each other, saying that they had found a Temple and again there were footsteps coming nearer across the courtyard.

Stanton Ware drew in his breath and wondered whether Zivana and he would find it hard to breathe in their hiding place.

Then he saw that in front of them at eye level there were small holes drilled beneath the hands of the Buddha.

They had been made so that they not only let in air but it was possible to see out through them into the Temple.

Drawing Zivana with him, he moved until they could look over the golden bowl with its sticks of incense and see the first of the Prince's men coming through the open doors.

There were four in front and many more struggling up the steps behind them.

Stanton Ware saw at once that they all carried the short curved Chinese swords which they usually wore in the belts of their coats.

They stood looking round them and he felt that for the moment they were a little awed by the silence and solemnity of the Temple and the huge golden statue of the Buddha.

Then just as he had appeared to them the Priest came from the shadows.

"What can I do for you, my sons?" he enquired.

His voice was mellow and deep with the intonation of a man, Stanton Ware knew, who practised the breathing that was part of the Lamas' training.

"We seek a man and a woman, Your Holiness," one of the men replied.

Now his awe, if that was what it had been, seemed to have abated and as he spoke he began to look round him, seeking his prey.

"A man?" the Priest questioned.

"A Mandarin, Your Holiness."

"And why should you come looking for him with weapons of war?"

"He has stolen from our Master, His Highness Prince Tuan, a valuable jewel."

"Indeed?" the Priest said coldly. "And why would he come here with it?"

"His life is forfeit for his treachery and because he has abused the laws of hospitality," the Prince's man said aggressively.

"And the woman?" the Priest asked.

"She is a concubine of no importance, but we have orders to take her back with us."

"Why should you expect such people to come to this Temple of the Lord Buddha?"

There was something stern in the way the Priest asked the questions and the man's eyes flickered and he looked embarrassed.

"We have been following them through the wood, Your Holiness. They cannot be very far away."

The Priest said nothing and another man came forward to ask,

"You have not seen the Mandarin?"

"I have seen no Mandarin," the Priest answered truthfully.

"They may have hidden themselves while you were at your prayers, Your Holiness."

"Then search for them, my son, if that is your wish," the Priest said. "But in this Holy place sheath your swords, for you all know as well as I do that the Lord Buddha forbade us to take life."

Somewhat sheepishly the Prince's men dipped their swords into their belts.

Then, not waiting for any further permission, they started moving round the Temple.

As the place was empty save for the great statue, it did not take them long and then they moved on to search the other buildings and courtyards.

But the Priest stood there silent and motionless in front of the golden statue as if their behaviour was of no interest and no concern of his.

Finally they returned to say,

"There is no sign of anyone here, Your Holiness."

The Priest merely inclined his head. Then, chattering to one another, the men ran down the steps of the Temple and disappeared into the darkness of the woods.

It was then as the last man reached the bottom step that Stanton Ware felt his tension relax and relief surge over him like a tidal wave.

He had watched through the small holes in the statue without moving, hardly breathing, knowing that if they were discovered there would be no hope for either him or Zivana.

As the breath that he had held so tightly left his lips in what was almost a sigh, Zivana turned towards him to fling herself against him.

His arms went round her and, as he held her close, he realised that she was trembling almost convulsively.

He did not speak, but pulled her closer and still closer as he had longed to do the night before.

Then she lifted her face to his and he realised that she was about to speak.

Stanton Ware was so experienced where intrigue was concerned and he had been in so many dangerous situations that he knew it was just fatal to assume that a search was over the moment the pursuers appeared to have left.

He was aware too that the Priest had made no movement to release them.

As he knew it was dangerous for either of them to make a sound and it was important that Zivana should not utter whatever words were trembling on her lips, he bent his head and his mouth came down on hers.

He had not really meant to kiss her, it was just an instinctive reaction to avoid danger.

Yet, as his lips touched hers, he knew it was what he had been longing for and what his body had ached for during all the long sleepless hours of the night.

For a moment he felt her stiffen in surprise.

Then, as he held her captive and her lips were very soft and innocent beneath his, he felt the instinctive movement of her hands, which had fluttered against his chest, cease and her body seemed to melt into his

Stanton Ware held her closer still and now something very strange and magical happened within him and he knew that this kiss was different from any he had given or received before in his whole life.

It was not only the danger that they had passed through which made it so intense, it was not only that Zivana was the most beautiful woman he had ever seen and he already loved her.

If was as if two souls who belonged to each other had met across Eternity and they were no longer two but one.

All that Stanton Ware had learnt in the Lamasery of the East had given him a heightened perception and understanding.

And in that very moment all that he believed of this world and the next was there when he claimed the woman who was already his as they had passed thousands of lives together.

The darkness of their hiding place had vanished and so they were together in the golden translucency of the Divine.

This was where they belonged not only because of their love in this life but because of their love and sacrifices in those that were past.

It flashed through Stanton Ware's mind that he was fortunate as few men were because he had found what he had always sought but had believed was impossible to find.

There was the scent of lilies and Zivana was no longer trembling.

He knew that instead she quivered with an awareness of the wonder that he himself was experiencing.

The exaltation and rapture he felt became more human as his lips became more insistent and more passionate, yet he knew she understood and he felt her respond.

How long they stood caught up in a wonder beyond words neither of them had any idea.

When at last Stanton Ware raised his head, he realised with a sense of shock where they were and knew that what had brought him down from the heights of utter bliss was that the Priest had moved.

He could hear his bare feet and then his voice saying,

"Your associates are by now some distance away. I suggest you join them."

His voice was cold and authoritative and, looking again through the holes in the statue, Stanton Ware saw two of the Prince's men emerging somewhat shamefacedly from the dark corner of the Temple.

"We were just making sure, Your Holiness, that the man we seek is not hiding in some fox's hole we have not searched," one of them said surlily.

"You defame this place," the Priest exclaimed. "Go!"

As if they were afraid he might curse them and all Chinese, whatever their religion may be, they are afraid of the curses of strange Priests and so the men hurried away.

They started to fall over each other as they ran down the steps and out into the wood.

Stanton Ware knew that he had been wise in preventing Zivana from speaking. At the same time in doing so he had found an inexpressible wonder and she knew that she felt the same.

She had made no attempt to move away from his arms, but had hidden her face against his shoulder as if she was shy.

They heard the faint click of the secret door behind them and it seemed to Stanton Ware as if the world encroached on the Heaven they had found for themselves within the sanctuary of the Buddha's body.

It was with reluctance that Zivana moved from the shelter of his arms to bend her head and go through the aperture and out into the narrow passage.

Stanton Ware followed her.

"How can I thank Your Holiness?" he asked the Priest.

"Come with me."

He walked ahead of them over the inner courtyard at the back of the Temple and entered a small building, which Stanton Ware realised was where he lived.

It was very simple, just one room, a table and a chair and a primitive stove.

At the far end of it stood a huge *K'ang* which stretched from wall to wall, on which a dozen monks or travellers could sleep if it was necessary.

The Priest closed the door and for the first time there was a faint smile on his thin lips as he said,

"You do not look, my son, as if you had a jewel of any great price on you."

"This is the jewel that they sought, Your Holiness," Stanton Ware said.

He indicated Zivana with his hand and she went down on her knees in front of the Priest and her forehead touched the ground.

"Rise, child," he said. "There is no more danger and I think as you have climbed a long way you must be thirsty."

"We are indeed," Stanton Ware agreed. "But we have a little food with us and we would be very gratified if Your Holiness would share it."

"As you must share mine," the Priest answered.

They sat down at the table and their meal consisted of what was left of the exotic foods which they had brought from The Palace and a soup made of vegetables and served with rice which Stanton Ware was sure came from one of the few devotees who attended the Temple,

There could not be many of them in this isolated spot and yet he knew that the Chinese would go many miles to worship at a Temple if they believed that it had special powers that would help them.

The Priest asked no questions and Stanton Ware respected him for his lack of curiosity, knowing it prevented him from having to invent falsehoods.

It was hard as they sat round the table for him to keep his eyes from Zivana.

She had taken her handkerchief from her head and laid it down beside her coolie hat.

He thought as the light flickered on her hair that she looked even more beautiful in her simple coolie dress than she had in the satins and jewels that she habitually wore.

She had a radiance about her that had not been there before and he knew it was because she loved him as he loved her.

After they had eaten, the Priest tidied away the dishes and said,

"I must go now to say my evening prayers, but I suggest, my children, that you stay here the night. Those men will continue to search for you for they will be afraid of returning to their Master without you."

"We would not wish you to run any risks on our behalf, Your Holiness," Stanton Ware said. "At the same time, since it will be cold outside, we would be grateful if we might avail ourselves of your hospitality."

"It will indeed be cold," the Priest answered, "and that is why I suggest that, while I am gone, you light the fire beneath the *K'ang*. I have a few kind people who wait upon me in the morning, but in the evening I am alone."

"I will do that," Stanton Ware replied.

The Priest smiled at them as he went from the building, closing the door behind him.

Stanton Ware looked at Zivana.

With a little murmur she ran towards him and hid her face against his shoulder.

"I was – frightened," she faltered in a soft voice, "terribly – terribly – frightened."

"And now that you are safe?" he asked.

"I am happy," she answered, "happy in a way I did not know it was possible to be."

He put his fingers under her chin and turned her face up towards his.

"Is it true that you love, me?" he asked. "I can hardly believe I am not imagining this."

"I love you," she whispered "but I did not know it until you – kissed me."

"I knew that I loved you last night," Stanton Ware said, "and it was an agony that I can never put into words to lie beside you and not touch you. I meant to wait and say nothing that would frighten or disturb you until I was sure that you loved me too."

He smiled as he said,

"I kissed you, my precious, to prevent you from betraying our hiding place to the men who I was sure were still listening outside."

"It was foolish of me not to think they might try to trick us," Zivana said humbly.

"I am glad you did not do so," Stanton Ware replied.

Her eyes fell before his and she murmured,

"So – am I."

He kissed her at first gently, then more passionately and once again Stanton Ware knew that this was different in every way from anything he had ever felt before.

"I love you, God knows I love you," he said. "And, my darling, you should never have been involved in a situation such as we are in now."

"I am not afraid," Zivana said. "Not when you hold me like this, but I was frightened last night. But now we are free of The Palace, I am alone with you and I know that you will look after me."

"That is what I want to do," Stanton Ware said with a little groan. "But then it will not be easy. We are a long way from Peking."

"Are you doubting your own strength and cunning?" Zivana asked him teasingly.

Then she added,

"How could I regret anything when I know now that we belong to each other? That I am a part of you?"

"Even though I am English?" he asked.

"You are just – you," she said softly, "and I was stupid to think that nationality could have anything to do with the real person I have been looking for all my life, although I did not realise it."

"I too thought that I would never find you," Stanton Ware said and his voice was deep.

As if he could not help himself, he kissed her once again, wildly and passionately, until her body moved against his and he knew he had awakened a fire within her to complement the raging furnace within himself.

"I love you! *I love you!*" Zivana cried. "But we must be – careful. I could not lose you now."

"We will win through," Stanton Ware said. "Can you doubt it when we were saved from destruction by the Lord Buddha Himself?"

"And because He gave us sanctuary," Zivana said in a very low voice, "He took us with Him into a glory that it was impossible to understand or even imagine."

"That is love," Stanton Ware replied, "the love that you and I have for each other, my perfect little pearl, my heart, my whole life!"

His voice now deepened and there was a highly possessive note of passion in it that she responded to as if he aroused music within her soul.

Then with an effort Stanton Ware took his arms from her.

"We must light the fire as our host has suggested," he said, "and tonight, my darling, we shall be well chaperoned and perhaps it is just as well!"

Zivana saw the expression in his eyes and blushed.

"You make me feel – shy," she answered, "but I think I shall be – cold unless I can lie – very close to you."

"It would be impossible for us to lie any other way," he replied, "but I wish that Yin had thought to provide us with warmer clothing than we have at the moment."

"It is enough for the daytime," Zivana said, "but at night – "

She shivered a little as she spoke for it was growing dusk quickly outside and, as she had anticipated, they could now feel the chill of snow in the air.

There was wood stacked in one corner of the room and Stanton Ware hurried to light the fire under the *K'ang*.

Zivana helped him to carry the logs and watched while he raked over the ashes to find that they were still warm from the night before.

He soon had a good fire burning, filling the room with the fragrance of pine.

As he turned to kiss Zivana for helping him, the door opened and the Priest returned.

He smiled at them benignly and then suggested,

"You must both be tired, so the sooner we sleep the better. Tomorrow morning there is a boy who comes early to bring me food before he goes to work. I will then find out from him whether it will be safe for you to proceed on your way."

"We are deeply grateful for your kindness," Stanton Ware said. "But for you I should at this moment be dead."

"And I should be in the – power of the – Prince," Zivana added and shuddered.

"I believe you were guided here," the Priest said, "and those whom the Enlightened One befriends are encompassed with the protection of His light."

"It is true," Stanton Ware said in all sincerity.

He and Zivana climbed onto the *K'ang*, which was by now growing warm and the Priest produced thick blankets woven by the peasants from wool that came from their Mongolian sheep.

They lay down in their clothes and the Priest did the same.

He chose the extreme end of the *K'ang* and turned his face to the wall. Zivana lay on the other side of it and Stanton Ware lowered himself next to her.

He tucked the rug round them both and then pulled Zivana close against him.

She put her head on his shoulder with a little sigh of happiness and he then kissed her forehead and her hair.

Then he deliberately let his mind wander in gratitude to their narrow escape.

He was quite sure that the Priest was right when he said that they had been guided to the Temple and that it was not by chance that their lives had been saved.

Stanton Ware had lived for too long in the East not to believe in the Fate that controlled everyone's life and he knew that the Karma of each individual twisted like a stream from birth until they were reborn.

He definitely knew now that in his past life his good deeds had brought him the wonder and perfection of Zivana and he thanked the Gods for her with his whole heart.

They were both more tired than they realised and neither Stanton Ware nor Zivana heard the Priest move from the *K'ang* soon after dawn and go to the Temple.

But, when he returned two hours later, he found them both awake and slightly ashamed to find that the sun had already risen and was glinting golden on the tiles in the courtyard.

The Priest came into the room and set a bowl of rice down on the table.

"I did not wish to awaken you," he said, "and I also thought it wisest for the boy who has brought our breakfast not to see you."

Stanton Ware got out of the *K'ang* to help the Priest prepare the water for the fragrant tea which they drank from little porcelain cups without handles.

As they sipped the hot liquid, the Priest told them,

"The boy informs me that there are many of the Prince's men in the forest. They slept beneath the trees and now they are moving about searching every nook and cranny."

"Will they come here again?" Stanton Ware asked.

"I think it most unlikely, except perhaps to enquire whether I have seen you," the Priest answered. "They are searching, my boy tells me, for a Mandarin."

"Which I am not, although I was dressed like one," Stanton Ware confessed.

The Priest did not answer and Stanton Ware was sure that he had been well aware of the truth from the beginning.

During the day when it was impossible for them to leave the safety of the small house, because Stanton Ware had thought it would please the Priest, he told him about the Lamasery where he had been taught.

He spoke of the wisdom he had learnt at the feet of one of the grand Lamas of how he had been permitted to use the secret sign that the Priest had recognised when they entered the Temple.

*

It was two days later before the Priest considered that it was safe for them to continue their journey.

Although it was a joy beyond words for them to be together, although they could kiss and be close to each other when they were alone, they were both acutely aware that it was important they should reach Peking as soon as possible.

The fact that they were in love did not exonerate them from fulfilling their mission and Stanton Ware was worried in case Yin had been unable to convey his message to Tseng-Wen and Mr. Herbert Squiers.

At the same time he did not wish to take any risks where Zivana was concerned.

On the third day the Priest agreed that on the morrow it would be reasonably safe for them to continue to move higher up on the mountains.

And the night before they were to leave he took them with him into the Temple where he said his evening prayers.

Because they knew that he wished it, Stanton Ware and Zivana knelt on either side of him in front of the giant golden Buddha.

There were more joss sticks than usual in the brass bowl and the air was heavy with the scent of incense.

Then, as the blue smoke curled upwards, Stanton Ware knew why the Priest had brought them there.

Through the smoke there was a glimmer of gold and the light from it swam in his brain. It grew larger and then there was a small picture like a scene through the reverse end of a telescope.

The picture moved, showing men marching and soldiers tramping steadily forward with Europeans and with them Japanese.

They were facing the towering walls of Peking and then, as they advanced, the great walls dissolved, crumbling before them to reveal purple, vermilion, and orange Pavilions.

Still the soldiers marched on and now Stanton Ware saw them enter Canal Street, where the British Legation stood with the Union Jack flying over it.

The doors were thrown open and there was a crowd of people rushing out, cheering, crying, waving, the women and children running to greet the troops.

Then there was darkness and only the blue smoke and the serene face of the Buddha,

The Priest had gone, but then, as Stanton Ware rose from his knees, Zivana flung herself against him,

"What did you see, my darling?" he asked and his voice was hoarse.

"I could see two – country carts leaving the – Imperial Palace by the Gate of Military Prowess," she whispered.

He did not speak and after a moment she went on,

"There was an elderly woman in one of them, wearing the coarse blue cotton dress of a peasant, but her face was black with anger."

Zivana paused and continued with an effort,

"It was the – Dowager Empress and with her was – the Emperor, wearing a common black robe, and also – Prince Tuan."

Stanton Ware drew in his breath. He understood what she had seen and it was linked with his own vision.

The Dowager Empress, the Emperor and their advisors would see from the City when the soldiers of the Great Powers marched in!

*

When morning came they set out, their plan being to keep to the mountains for at least two days and then to drop down into the Peking valley and approach the City from a direction that anyone watching for them would not be expecting.

It sounded very easy when they talked about it, but, when they set off walking, it was as difficult as it had been before and Stanton Ware was anxious in case it should prove too much for Zivana.

She was, however, very much tougher than she looked and she told him that unlike most Chinese women she exercised herself every day and had learnt Yoga and practised it both mentally and physically.

It certainly stood her in good stead as they journeyed over the mountains, sometimes dropping down into deep ravines only to be obliged to then climb up the other side.

There were paths above deep gorges that were so slippery and so dangerous that Stanton Ware was terrified that she might fall.

They spent the first night in a cave. It was very cold, although they cuddled up to each other and Stanton Ware had carried on his back a blanket that the Priest had given them.

He had left a large gift of money behind when they departed.

He knew, if he offered it directly to the Priest, it would be refused, so instead he hid it on the table under an upturned teacup.

The Priest had blessed them and there had been sincerity both in his words and his voice, which after they had left made Zivana say,

"Now I know that we shall get home safely."

Stanton Ware, looking at the happiness in her eyes, wanted to believe her.

The first danger came when they dropped down into the plain and, finding a farmer who kept animals, tried to bargain with him for two of his horses.

He refused their request, saying he needed the animals for himself, but suggested another farmer who might oblige.

Although it meant a detour of some miles, Stanton Ware thought it was worth the effort.

From a surly man who was more Mongolian than Chinese they managed to buy two old horses that he had no further use for.

They were slow and obstinate, but at least they rested Zivana's feet.

Although she had said nothing, Stanton Ware could see that her toes were bleeding from climbing over the sharp-edged rocks.

Because he was frightened of her being once again in danger, he insisted on their making a long detour before they turned towards Peking.

They slept in many strange places, in barns that were empty as the crops had not yet been brought in and in an inn, which was cleaner and less crowded than they usually were.

One night, as they were now away from the snows and it was very hot in the daytime and warm after dark, they slept under the shadows of some weeping-willow trees, which threw a green protective tent over them and the leaves seemed to whisper the music of love.

It was as they neared the City that they came upon the Boxers, who were everywhere.

In every crowd, in every village, moving along the road, camping out in the fields, there was the flash of scarlet and every available wall was plastered with posters.

Stanton Ware tried to avoid contact with them, but once when he and Zivana had to stop to buy some food in a small village, unexpectedly a dozen Boxers appeared.

Ragged, dirty and aggressive, they wore their scarlet headscarves and sashes with the air of those who possess immortality.

Hurriedly Stanton Ware paid for the purchases he had made and would have remounted his horse when a Boxer stopped him.

He was a well-built young man of nineteen or twenty years of age with a pockmarked face and hair falling almost to his shoulders.

"Where are you going?" he asked.

"My wife and I, sir, are taking these horses back to the farmer who owns them," Stanton Ware replied. "Then, if we may, we would like to come back into the village and then see a demonstration, if you are giving one."

He spoke both eagerly and humbly and the Boxer looked pleased.

"You'll have to hurry," he said. "The people are collecting for one now."

"We will be very quick," Stanton Ware said.

The Boxer looked towards Zivana.

She had bent her head so that her face was hidden by her large-brimmed coolie hat.

Stanton Ware saw the man's eyes flicker over her slim figure and felt a sudden stab of fear that was almost like the thrust of a dagger.

The Boxer moved towards her.

"Let's have a look at your wife," he said. "There's a shortage of women round here."

Stanton Ware was very still.

He could knock down the Boxer, he knew, without any difficulty, but there were others within earshot and he was quite certain that they would avenge any act of violence.

"Let's have a look at you," the Boxer said to Zivana.

She raised her head and, if the Boxer was surprised, so was Stanton Ware.

Zivana's eyes were turned inwards to her nose in a monstrous squint and her mouth was twisted sideways in a gross grimace that was revolting.

The Boxer stepped back.

"Get on with you," he said roughly. "You'll have to hurry not to miss the magic."

"We will be back," Stanton Ware said, flinging himself into the saddle.

They rode on and gradually his heart began to beat normally.

When they were clear of the village, he turned to Zivana,

"How did you do that? How did you make yourself look like that?"

She laughed and it was a sound of sheer amusement.

"When I was staying in the Forbidden City," she replied, "there was a eunuch who we all hated and some of the girls and I used to make faces at him behind his back. When the others laughed, he was always mystified as to what had amused them."

Stanton Ware laughed too. At the same time he was determined to take no more risks, and if they had to go hungry before they reached Peking it was much better than coming into further contact with the Boxers.

As they came to the centre of the valley, they saw a burning building and Zivana gave a little exclamation.

"Do you know which that one is?" she asked.

"I am not certain," Stanton Ware replied.

"It is the British Summer Legation."

"There is no need for us to ask who has burnt it to the ground," he said harshly.

He felt that this was the beginning of the war they had feared and he only prayed that Herbert Squiers had received his message and that Sir Claude Macdonald was at last alert to the danger of what might be happening.

It was, however, impossible for them to reach Peking that night and so they slept in the shade of some trees in what was the private Park of a Minister's Summer Palace.

They did not go near the house, but Stanton Ware had the idea that it was shuttered and barred and he wondered how many people were fortifying themselves against the aggression of the Boxers.

*

The following day they moved nearer to the City and now there were great congregations of Boxers everywhere they looked.

There were also Chinese who had come out from the City to stare open-mouthed at them, calling for demonstrations and being utterly convinced that every magic trick was completely genuine.

It was really impossible to count the number of red headscarves and sashes they saw, but Stanton Ware thought that there were more than anyone had ever anticipated.

Although they might well be a ragged, illiterate uncouth lot, Prince Tuan could count on a large following.

In the afternoon of the next day as they were nearing the City, they could see that on the outskirts there were several Churches on fire.

Stanton Ware avoided going near them and, keeping to the side-streets, they hurried their horses as best they could into the quarter where Tseng-Wen's house stood.

It had taken them all day to reach Peking and it was growing dusk when finally they dismounted, not at the main door of the Mansion but at one which Zivana said was used by the servants.

They had decided that this was advisable because, as Stanton Ware said,

"There is always the chance that Prince Tuan will by now be in Peking and waiting for you to return home. If he has set men to watch the house, you could be spirited away before we can even knock on the door."

"You think of everything," she replied softly, a caressing note in her voice.

"I am trying to think of you," he answered her. "In fact I can think of nothing else but particularly of your safety."

"We will not say that you have actually succeeded until we are indoors," she said with a smile.

But, as Stanton Ware dismounted to then knock on the side door, he noted with some satisfaction that the street was empty.

He knocked but there was no answer, then with an anxious look at Zivana he knocked again.

There was a long wait and he was just about to knock for the third time when there were sounds of bolts being removed and a face peeped out.

It was Yin!

Zivana jumped down from her horse.

"You are back, Yin!" she cried out. "Thank goodness you are safe. We have been very worried about you."

"And I about you, Mistress," Yin answered.

He hurried them inside and then took their horses to the stables.

Stanton Ware followed Zivana through two courtyards until they came to the house.

Even as they entered he was sure that Tseng-Wen was not there.

The place felt empty and sure enough, when Yin returned, he said,

"The Master has gone away."

"Where to?" Zivana asked.

"To stay with his Honourable brother twenty miles to the East. The Master very worried when I gave him your message, Noble Sir," he said to Stanton Ware, "and he went to The Palace to talk with Li Hung-Chang."

"I am glad about that," Stanton Ware commented.

"When the Master returned," Yin went on, "he thought because of the way His Highness the Prince had behaved it would be best for him to leave Peking."

Zivana looked at Stanton Ware.

"I am sure that was wise," she said in a low voice. "The Prince might have tried to hurt him."

Stanton Ware nodded.

"I have stayed behind," Yin said, "waiting for you, Noble Sir, and my Mistress to arrive. Now I am very happy to see you."

"We are very happy to be here," Zivana replied, "and I am really longing for a change of clothes!"

"What I would suggest, Mistress," Yin said respectfully, "is that you do not stay in the house. I have sent the servants away, but the Prince might still be watching."

"That is what you anticipated," Zivana remarked to Stanton Ware.

"Where can we go?" he asked.

"To the Lotus Pavilion at the bottom of the garden," Yin answered. "It is very quiet there and I will look after you."

Zivana clapped her hands.

"That is a splendid idea, Yin. Very few people know that the Lotus Pavilion even exists."

She put her hand into Stanton Ware's.

"Come and look," she said. "Tseng-Wen built it for his wife many years ago. No one has lived in it since she died and it is very beautiful. A place that was made for love."

She spoke the last words so that only Stanton Ware could hear them and, as he looked into her eyes, his fingers tightened on hers.

CHAPTER SIX

Down the garden behind weeping-willow trees that obscured it from the house there was a white Pavilion with artificial canals surrounding it on both sides.

It was reached only by a narrow arched bridge and, as soon as he saw it, Stanton Ware knew that Zivana had been right when she said that it had been made for love.

The walls were of fine carved lattice-work and the roof had *griffons* at each corner to ward off evil spirits.

The water on either side of the Pavilion was thick with lotus flowers just opening in all the pure loveliness of their white petals.

When Stanton Ware crossed the bridge and had entered the Pavilion, he thought it was a perfect frame for Zivana's beauty. There were only two rooms, the first and larger appeared to be a sitting room, until one noticed the curtains that covered one end.

Of almond-blossom pink, they were embroidered with endless flowers and, when drawn back, revealed a large *K'ang* covered with a silken mattress.

The other room was smaller and more masculine, containing a magnificent collection of green jade, which was believed by the Chinese to have magical qualities.

"We shall be very happy here," Zivana said softly.

It was an effort for him to reply firmly,

"First I need a bath and then I know that we are both hungry."

He looked at Yin as he was speaking and, as the servant hurried away to prepare dinner for them, Stanton Ware went to his own room.

He was right in saying that they were both hungry for the last two days, as they neared Peking, they had been afraid because of the Boxers to go into the marketplaces of the villages they passed through.

They had been able to buy only a little rice and a few vegetables from peasants who were nervous of what was about to happen in the City and so were hiding their food.

They had ridden for hours each day and, although they could not travel fast as the horses were such poor specimens, it had been very tiring in the heat.

It had resulted in their falling asleep almost as soon as they lay down each night.

Although he held Zivana in his arms, Stanton Ware had forced himself not to think of love but only of the danger that they both were in.

He had the feeling, just as she had, that the Priest with his inner vision would not have set them on their journey if he had not been sure that they would reach their destination.

He found himself, as they travelled on, thinking about the Priest and at times feeling his presence so vividly that he knew he was at that moment praying for them.

One night whilst they lay in a barn on a pile of grasses that the farmer had gathered as fodder for his horses, he was worrying silently about Zivana.

Her head moved against his shoulder and she said softly,

"There is no need. We are in the hands of the Enlightened One."

He was not surprised that she should know just what he was thinking for then already their thoughts were so attuned to each other's that sometimes they communicated without any words being said aloud.

There was a calm confidence in her voice.

Without replying he kissed her gently and, almost before he raised his lips from hers, she was asleep.

In his room in the Lotus Pavilion, Stanton Ware said a prayer of thanks and gratitude for their safe arrival.

Though Zivana had been confident, he himself had passed through many agonies of fear.

He realised that not only did her beauty constitute a danger, but there was a chance that they might be taken for Christian Chinese.

In the Provinces the Boxers had killed hundreds of Christians and it was only because it was difficult to assess their numbers and there was no national outcry about it that members of the Legations had not thought it serious.

The reports that Stanton Ware had studied told him that the Boxers were just as violently opposed to the Chinese who had turned Christian as they were to the foreigners.

Fortunately many of the young hooligans were so ignorant that the only method they had of gauging whether a Chinese was Christian or not was to look for the cross they expected to find on their foreheads.

Many people escaped death because of this, but a number of others were killed because the villagers denounced them or because the Boxers just wanted to be brutal.

But here Zivana was safe. And Stanton Ware felt himself relax as the scented bathwater soaked away the fears that had beset him both night and day since they had left the Temple.

He did not hurry and, when he then went into Zivana's room, she had already changed and was waiting for him.

She was looking exquisitely beautiful in a gown of soft pink, the colour of the curtains over her *K'ang*. There were diamonds and sapphires in her hair and round her wrists and her nail protectors flashed with the same stones.

These, as they both knew, were just an affectation for she had cut her nails when she had assumed the garb of a coolie.

Stanton Ware stood looking at her and for a moment neither of them could move.

Their eyes met and so, without touching each other, they knew that they were close in an indescribable manner, which held them captive to their love.

Then, as she looked away from his eyes to what he was wearing, Zivana exclaimed,

"You are going out!"

She saw that Stanton Ware was not dressed in one of the embroidered Mandarin's robes which Tseng-Wen had given him to play his part in The Palace.

These clothes had been waiting for him in the Lotus Pavilion with his own European clothes which he had left in Peking.

Yin, when he came to him after preparing dinner, had told him that, when the Prince's servants had gone rushing up the mountain, he had turned the baggage cart round and set off in it for Peking.

"That was clever of you, Yin," Stanton Ware said with a smile.

"Nothing is lost, except the clothes in the deep hole," Yin had replied proudly. "When everything is quiet, I will go back to collect them."

But Stanton Ware had refused to look at his Mandarin garments and instead had dressed himself in a plain cheap cotton robe that Yin had procured for him.

It was the type of garment that would be worn by the keeper of a small shop or by a clerk and he knew that, if he passed anyone in the street, they would not give him a second glance.

He heard both regret and a touch of fear in Zivana's voice and he went to her to take her gently in his arms.

"I love you!" he said, "and soon there will be time to tell you of the depth, height and breadth of my love. But first I must do what we both know is my duty."

She gave a little sigh that seemed to come from the very depths of her being before she said softly,

"You know I understand."

He kissed her forehead, then they drew apart as they heard Yin coming over the bridge, a tray of food in his hands.

They sat down on a low silken couch and the food that Yin had prepared would at any time have tasted delicious, but it was now doubly so because they both ravenously hungry.

There was fresh fish prepared with a sweet and sour sauce, which Stanton Ware always enjoyed and there were small plump birds, slivers of pork, other meats and chicken and the richness of turtle flesh to finish the meal.

Only when they had eaten for nearly an hour did they feel replete.

Stanton Ware sat back against the cushions and raised his glass of Samshu to his lips.

"I am beginning to feel more human," he announced.

Zivana laughed.

"So am I and I must admit that all today my mind kept wandering towards the food when I should have been thinking of higher things."

"I was thinking only of you," Stanton Ware said. "But at the same time, my darling, I admit that I was extremely hungry."

She put out her hand towards him.

"It is so wonderful to be here," she said softly, "and with – you."

He held her hand tightly in his as he asked,

"How would you wish to be married, my precious? As a Chinese, as a Russian or as the wife of an Englishman?"

He felt her stiffen for a moment as if he startled her, then there was a radiance in her eyes that was unmistakable.

"It does not – matter how I am – married," she answered, "as long as I become – your wife."

"That is what I hoped you would say," Stanton Ware replied.

He rose to his feet and drew her into his arms.

"I shall be as quick as I can, my sweet one," he said, "and, when I return, we will make plans for our Wedding tomorrow. It will be a very quiet Ceremony."

"The only thing that matters is that you should be there," Zivana replied.

"And you," he answered.

He kissed her until the Lotus Pavilion seemed to swim dizzily around them.

Then he went away without looking back, knowing that if he did it would be even harder for him to go.

*

"I can hardly believe it is really you," Herbert Squiers said as Stanton Ware sat with him in the American Legation.

"You received my communication?"

"The moment your servant handed me the information about the Boxers, I put pressure on my Minister to call a meeting with Sir Claude Macdonald."

"And then what happened?"

"The Legations had all sunk into their usual lethargy after a contingent of troops arrived on June first."

"They came here?" Stanton Ware exclaimed.

He knew that they had been sent because of the urgent telegram he had despatched to the Foreign Office immediately on his arrival.

Herbert Squiers nodded.

"There were seventy-five Russians, the same number each of British and French, fifty American Marines, forty Italians and thirty-five Japanese."

"That will not be enough," Stanton Ware added quickly.

"I realised that when I received your message," Herbert Squiers said, "and Sir Claude Macdonald, on the insistence of my Minister, sent an urgent telegram to Admiral Sir Edward Seymour."

"Who was in the warship at Taku."

"Correct. Nearly two thousand men left Tientsin on the following day by train, but they encountered the Boxers halfway between Tientsin and Peking."

"There was fighting?"

"The trains were attacked by a large force of Boxers," Herbert Squiers explained. "They believed their incantations and faith would prevent foreign bullets and foreign swords from hurting them."

"They have actually come to trust their own tricks," Stanton Ware murmured.

"Hie troops opened fire and killed about fifty Boxers," Herbert Squiers carried on. "The rest ran away, but the Dowager Empress learnt that there were foreign troops approaching the Capital."

"The Boxers will move in here tomorrow," Stanton Ware asserted,

"The Imperial troops will do everything possible to prevent Sir Edward Seymour from coming to our rescue."

"That is obvious," Stanton Ware replied, "and I think you will find it impossible to move outside the Legations."

He was thinking of the vision he had seen in the Temple when he went on,

"As you will know, the most easily defended is the British. I have a feeling that you will eventually all be besieged there."

He saw the astonishment in Herbert Squiers's eyes.

Then he said quietly,

"One thing that is very important is that you should have ample supplies of food."

"You are absolutely right," Herbert Squiers agreed. "Even if Sir Edward Seymour arrives before there is such a siege, it would be foolish not to take every precaution."

"Exactly," Stanton Ware agreed.

He rose as he spoke, then, as he was about to bid the First Secretary farewell, he asked,

"Do you know how I could get in touch with a Russian Priest?"

"I think it most unlikely that one would venture outside the Legation at the moment, they are far too distinctive in their black robes and long beards," Herbert Squiers replied. "Many Churches were burnt today on the outskirts of the City and I am certain that, if the Boxers arrive tomorrow, the rest will suffer the same fate."

Stanton Ware said no more.

As he walked back from the Legation through the crowded streets where there was an undeniable atmosphere of fear, he thought it was going to be difficult to marry Zivana at once as he had intended.

Without consciously thinking about it, he sent out an inner cry for help, which he always used when it was a case of emergency.

He wanted Zivana to belong to him, he had the feeling that he would be able to protect her as his wife even more effectively than he could do at the moment.

As he walked on, he became aware that underneath the rags or cotton robes of many of the men moving about the streets there was a touch of scarlet.

It was only a glimpse here and there, but enough to make Stanton Ware know that many of the Boxers had not waited for the orders from Prince Tuan but were already in the City.

He was certain that this was so when he smelt burning and saw men hurrying through the gloom with bundles under their arms.

Already, he thought, the looting has begun.

He guessed that the fires would be in the premises of the traders who were known to be foreign, but he knew it always happened that once a fire had been lit it was very difficult to confine it and not only the foreign traders but also the Chinese would suffer.

A man came out of a side-turning and almost knocked him over. He was weighted down by what he carried in his arms.

As he moved quickly away, disappearing into the shadows, Stanton Ware felt something beneath his foot and bent down automatically to pick it up.

It was difficult to see in the dim light of the street, but he felt by its shape that it was the Imperial Emblem of the Five-Clawed Dragon holding a pearl.

Originally it was the symbol of the fertilising rain it had been taken as the emblem of the Imperial Family and was to be seen throughout the Palaces. It had become a symbol of China itself struggling to seize the flaming pearl of all knowledge and Power.

This was only a small reproduction of the huge Dragons found everywhere on the walls in the Forbidden City and decorating also all of the Civic buildings.

Stanton Ware slipped it into his pocket and hurried on, keeping to the more unfrequented alleys and streets until he came within sight of Tseng-Wen's house.

It was then that he heard a sharp cry and then saw just ahead of him some men straggling together. He moved quickly to one side to avoid them.

Then he looked again and saw that two youths. and he was certain they were Boxers, had knocked an old man to the ground.

They were shouting at him, "Christian! *Christian!*" together with a number of foul words in a dialect he recognised as coming from the Province of Shantung.

Without thinking of his own safety, Stanton Ware moved forward and a second later the youths, staggering under his blows, were running away as fast as their legs could carry them.

He bent down to help to his feet the man who they had been assaulting.

For a moment he appeared to be unconscious.

Then, as Stanton Ware lifted him up, he groaned and said in Chinese but with a foreign accent,

"Thank you for your kindness to an old man."

It was hard to see his face, but he was obviously finding it hard to breathe and Stanton Ware, having seen the glint of steel, was sure that one of the Boxers had attacked him with a knife.

"My house is near here," he said. "Let us seek shelter while you regain your breath."

He knocked on the side door and almost immediately it was opened by Yin.

He looked with surprise at the man whom Stanton Ware was almost carrying in his arms.

"Boxers!" Stanton Ware said briefly.

As he assisted the man inside the door, Yin shut it behind them and locked and bolted it.

The lights were lit in the small room at the back of the house and, as Stanton Ware set the old man down in a chair, he saw that he had a long beard.

He was wearing a cloak and the hood covered his head, but now, as it fell back, one glance at the high cheekbones and the dark eyes told Stanton Ware that the man who he had rescued was not only a Russian but also a Priest!

He knew that here was the answer to his cry for help, which he had sent out as he walked back through the City.

As he wiped the blood from a cut on the Priest's face, he thought that the Power to which he had appealed had never failed him.

After a glass of Samshu, the Russian was able to talk and then, when he had thanked his rescuer with every expression of gratitude, Stanton Ware said,

"May I suggest, Father, that it is most unwise to walk about the streets? The Boxers have infiltrated the City and tomorrow there will be thousands of them converging on Peking to burn the Churches and kill not only foreigners but all the Chinese Christians they can find."

"My Church was burnt today," the Russian Priest replied, "but I took the members of my staff and many of the congregation who are Chinese into a cellar near here where we are safe. But we have little food and not much money."

He gave a sigh.

"I was trying to reach the Russian Legation to ask for help, but I realise now we should have foreseen that this might happen and made provision long ago."

"You are only one of many who shut their eyes to what might occur," Stanton Ware said, "and now you will never reach the Legation."

"I realise that," the Priest said with a sigh.

"I will give you food and money," Stanton Ware went on. "You must send one of your Chinese out to buy what you require, but if you value your life do not come out of the cellar until the foreign troops arrive."

Now the Priest looked at him and asked,

"Why should you help us?"

"Shall I say because I am a Christian?"

The Priest seemed to accept this as an explanation and next Stanton Ware said,

"Before you leave, Father, may I ask a favour?"

"You saved my life, my son," the Priest replied. "Anything I can do for you is yours for the asking."

"I wish to be married to someone who has been baptised into your Church," Stanton Ware said quietly.

"It will be a pleasure," the Priest answered.

"I would like first to wash and change my clothes," Stanton Ware said to Yin. "Will you take this Holy man to your Mistress and explain that we are to be married immediately?"

"That is good news, Noble Sir, very good news," Yin exclaimed with delight.

Stanton Ware hurried to the Lotus Pavilion.

He crossed the bridge and, as he did so, he saw the lights in Zivana's room and knew that she was waiting for him.

He did not wish to go to her dressed in the low-grade garments in which he had passed without comment through the City and he felt dirty from the crowds and from contact with the Boxers.

It took him a little time to wash and, while he was wondering just what he should wear, wishing he could be married in his own clothes, Yin appeared with a robe over his arm.

"This is a Chinese Wedding garment, Noble Sir," he said. "It is what Tseng-Wen wore on his own Wedding day and I know that he would want you to wear it at yours when you are married to the Mistress who is so close to his heart."

Stanton Ware thought that this was true and he saw as well that the robe was exquisitely embroidered with all the emblems of good luck and happiness.

"Perhaps it is best that the Priest should continue to think I am a Chinese," he said aloud, almost as if he was speaking, to himself.

"*'Unnecessary risk can be a two-edged dagger',*" Yin quoted.

"That is true," Stanton Ware agreed. "You have told the Mistress?"

"She is very happy," Yin smiled, "and she make preparations even though there is little time."

As Stanton Ware, gloriously arrayed in the beautiful Manchu Wedding garment, went into Zivana's room, he understood what these preparations entailed.

Everywhere there were candles flickering against the carved walls of the Pavilion and from the other courtyards Yin had brought in great bowls of lilies, which scented the air.

Floating gently among the lotuses on the waters of the canals outside were the little boats of good wishes that the Chinese always lit on special occasions to bring good luck.

Flickering candles tied to fragile pieces of bamboo floated out into the darkness just like prayers.

It was all very beautiful, but, as he looked at Zivana, Stanton Ware drew in his breath.

She too had changed and her gown was white, embroidered with butterflies, each wing embellished with jewels.

There were pearls and diamonds in her hair and a long string of perfect pearls falling from her neck to her waist.

Her eyes were very large and dark in her small face and they held, Stanton Ware thought, not only happiness but also the mystery and wonder of the ages.

As he advanced towards her, she held out her hand and, walking side by side they moved towards the Priest, who stood at the far end of the room waiting for them.

They went down on their knees before him and he married them in Russian according to the rites of the Russian Orthodox Church.

The prayers were those which Stanton Ware had repeated when he was young and, when they took their vows, he knew that the words were exactly the same in any language as they dedicated themselves to each other and to God.

Stanton Ware had no ring to give Zivana, but she gave him one of hers which was made of the purest jade.

As he slipped it on her finger, he knew that the unbroken circle was symbolic of the life they would live together and that they were part of each other now and for all Eternity.

The Priest blessed them and, as Zivana's fingers tightened on Stanton Ware's, he knew that for a moment in time their souls soared free of their bodies into the indefinable space of the Divine.

Although there might be many trials and difficulties ahead, their love would protect them and they need never be afraid.

As they then rose from their knees, the Priest turned away without speaking as if he was aware how Holy the moment had been for them.

Yin escorted him across the arched bridge and back through the courtyards to the house, where the food and the money he had been promised was waiting.

When he had gone and there was no longer any sound in the Pavilion, but only a silence that seemed filled with glory, Zivana looked up at Stanton Ware as he stood beside her.

"You are my wife," he said softly.

There was a touch of wonder in his voice as if he could hardly believe it to be true.

"And you are my husband," she answered gently.

"I love you because you are a woman," he said, "I revere you because you are sacred to me and I worship you because you are not only of this world but also a part of the Divine."

He spoke slowly and his voice was very deep.

Then, as Zivana looked up into his eyes, he thought that hers filled with tears before she knelt down in front of him and her forehead touched the floor at his feet.

"No, no!" he said quickly and then, bending down, picked her up to hold her close in his arms.

"It is how I feel about you," she said, "as you are so magnificent – so wonderful that I am as humble as any Chinese woman might be before her Master."

"My precious ridiculous darling," Stanton Ware said hoarsely.

Now the spell that had held them apart broke and his mouth found hers.

He kissed her with slow demanding kisses as if he sought to draw her very soul from between her lips and make it his.

"I love you!" Zivana said. "I love you so much that I am afraid this is all a dream and I shall awaken to find that we are still a long way from home."

"It is no dream," Stanton Ware replied, "except that you are not really human! You are in fact everything perfect in Chinese art. You are like the magic of jade and the translucence of porcelain and you have the inner perfection and significance of their paintings."

He kissed her again as he spoke and Zivana said,

"We have been married as Russians."

"That is a part of you I intend to discover later."

He felt a little quiver go through her and he knew that it was because she responded to the passion in his voice.

"But really I am English," she said, "the wife of an Englishman."

"Do you resent that?" Stanton Ware enquired.

"Never! *Never!*" she cried. "I am so proud and happy. I am thrilled to belong to you and I take back all I have ever said or thought about the English, because if you are

~162~

typical of its countrymen than it must be the most perfect place in the world!"

Stanton Ware laughed and then he said,

"This is our Wedding night, my darling, and the only thing I regret is that I have nothing to give you and even your ring already belonged to you."

"Does it matter?" Zivana asked softly.

"Not in the least!" he answered. "But wait, I have remembered something."

He put his hand into his pocket as he spoke and drew out the little dragon emblem, which he had transferred when he had changed from his cheap robe.

When he had seen it in the light, he knew that in fact it must be extremely valuable and that he had been so right in thinking that the Boxers had been looting the richest quarter of Peking where the furriers, the antique dealers, the jewellers and silk merchants all had their shops.

The Imperial Emblem that he had picked up from the mud was of *cloisonné* enamel and the Dragon's head was of gold and so were its five claws and raised foot.

As he held it out to Zivana, Stanton Ware saw that the flaming pearl of all knowledge and power was of a soft translucent pink and perfect in shape. It was in fact one of the finest pearls he had ever seen in China.

"Where did you find this?" Zivana asked.

"Lying in the road," Stanton Ware replied.

"It had been looted?"

"It must have been. It could have come from one of the expensive jewellers or perhaps a private house, but, wherever it came from, it would be impossible for us to return it."

"So you would give it to me."

"It is my Wedding present, my darling," he said with a smile.

"It could not be more suitable," she answered.

He looked at her.

Then he understood.

"Of course." he said. "You are the Perfect Pearl and I am the Dragon who will hold you, defend you and keep you safe from danger."

"That is what I thought," she said. "It must have been meant that you should find this emblem tonight of all nights."

"My precious perfect little pearl," Stanton Ware whispered.

He put his arms around her and then with one hand he drew the jewelled pins from her hair.

He threw them down carelessly on the couch beside them and, as Zivana's long black tresses fell over her shoulders, reaching almost to her waist, he buried his face in them.

"This is what I have longed for," he said hoarsely. "I have wanted to see you ever since I kissed you in the body of Buddha."

"Why did you not – release it – before?" Zivana asked.

She found it hard to speak because the thrills he evoked were rippling through her.

"Because I was keeping a strict control over myself," Stanton Ware replied. "It has been hard, my darling, when you are so beautiful."

His voice deepened as he went on,

"Everything about you not only sends my heart soaring into the Heavens but makes my body ache and long for you in a way that I cannot describe."

He kissed her hair again, feeling the silkiness of it against his lips, before he said,

"I have been so afraid of frightening you or making you feel that I was taking advantage of our situation. But now tonight you are mine and I can love to you as I have wanted to do so much."

"And as – I have – wanted you to," Zivana whispered

Her words inflamed him and his kisses became fiercer and more demanding.

He felt as if he was indeed a Dragon holding a pearl beyond price within his grasp and defying the whole world to take it from him.

He kissed her until her body trembled against his and he knew that the fire within him had awakened a flame within her so that her lips clung to his and her arms drew him even closer.

He picked her up and carrying her high against his heart crossed the room to the *K'ang*.

He pulled back the almond-blossom curtains with all their magnolia embroidery and laid Zivana down on the soft mattress, her dark hair flowing over the pillows.

As she lay there looking at him, he stood for a moment without moving before he said,

"When you came to me in the Prince's Palace, you came in all humility as a Chinese woman approaches a man, starting at the foot of the bed and rising slowly towards him."

Zivana made a little murmur and he went on before she could speak,

"That is why, my darling, because tonight I approach you in the same way, I shall first kiss your feet as I knew how much you had suffered when we walked so far. But you never complained and I love you even more for it."

He bent down as he spoke and kissed her small toes one after another, then the arched instep of each foot.

Zivana's skin was very soft, as soft, he thought, as the petals of the lotus flowers on the water outside the Pavilion.

He drew off his robe and, as he moved onto the *K'ang*, Zivana's arms were round his neck, drawing him towards her and her lips were ready for his.

He swept her dark hair away first from one of her small ears, then from the other, kissing them until he heard her breath come quickly between her lips and he knew at once that he was exciting her.

Once again her mouth was lifted towards his, but he kissed her forehead and ran his lips over the winged eyebrows that were a perfect frame for the mystery of her eyes.

"You are so perfect," he said, "and every little part of you belongs to me."

He looked down at her to say,

"I shall be jealous of the very air that you breathe, the birds you listen to, the flowers you touch. You are mine, mine completely and absolutely and I will share you with nothing and no one!"

"There is – nothing else in this – world but – you."

He felt her arms drawing his head down and her body arching as she wanted him closer than he was already. Still he avoided her lips and kissed first her small nose, her pointed chin and then the corner of her mouth.

He knew now that the fires within her were rising higher. He could feel her whole body trembling against his as the pressure of her arms became more insistent.

Then at last his mouth took hers captive.

He knew as their lips touched that they were swept away as they had been before into a wonder and glory that was so rapturous and so perfect, that the ecstasy of it was almost too poignant to be borne.

Yet Stanton Ware was human, a man who loved spiritually with all the sensitivity of a higher intelligence, but also indeed with the physical passion that is the power and source of life itself.

He knew as he drew Zivana closer and still closer, until they were no longer two people but one, that he had in fact found the perfect precious pearl who he had sought all his life.

A pearl which for most people was always out of reach, but was the love that came from the Gods themselves, the love of enlightenment.

*

Morning brought the song of the birds in the garden, the sun glinting golden on the canal and the scent of lilies mingling with the fragrance that came from flowers in the courtyards.

Lying half-asleep with Zivana in his arms, Stanton Ware thought that his contentment enveloped him to the point where it was difficult to believe that he was still on earth.

Although he had not moved, Zivana must have indeed sensed that he was awake for after a moment she asked him,

"Are you – happy?"

"That is the question I intended to ask you, my darling."

"I could not believe such happiness existed or that any man could be so wonderful – so strong and yet so gentle," she answered.

"*You* are perfect," he said as he had said a thousand times during the night.

She moved from the circle of his arms to step down from the *K'ang,* pulling a robe over her body and lifting her dark hair back from her shoulders with a gesture that was as exquisite as that of a bird in flight.

"It is morning," she exclaimed as if she was surprised.

"Has the night been too long or too short?" Stanton Ware asked, watching her.

"Much, much too short," she answered. "It has sped by on winged feet – and now there is another day – and we can never have yesterday again."

"Would you like to do?" he enquired.

"Yesterday or rather last night – my Wedding day was just so perfect that I want to hold onto it with both hands and not let the wonder of it escape me."

"There will be many other days and nights," he said. "Thousands of them when we will be together."

"I know," she said, "and each one will be more precious and perfect than the last."

She was smiling at him as they heard the soft footsteps of Yin approaching the Pavilion and Stanton Ware rose from the *K'ang*.

"I bring news to the Mistress," Yin said, bowing to Zivana.

"What is it?" she asked, a little note of fear in her voice.

"The Boxers have entered the City. They are everywhere. They are beginning to burn the Churches and the foreign compounds."

Zivana moved towards Stanton Ware as if for protection and he put his arm around her.

"Two Roman Catholic Churches are in flames," Yin said, "the American Presbyterian Mission and many others."

"And the people?" Stanton Ware asked.

"They are all frightened. The Boxers are making a lot of noise and threatening to murder any Chinese who may try to stop them. And they are killing every Chinese who they think is a. Christian."

"What is happening in the Forbidden City?" Stanton Ware asked.

"It is difficult to find out for certain, Noble Sir," Yin replied, "but it is rumoured that the Empress has ordered the Army to go to the railroad area to prevent the advance of the foreign troops."

"This then means war!" Stanton Ware said quietly.

Zivana gave a little cry.

"Can nothing stop them?"

"I am afraid not."

Later on in the day, although Zivana tried to prevent him, Stanton Ware insisted on going to find out what had occurred.

He knew it would be quite impossible without danger to go near the American or British Legations and he then decided that the best thing he could do would be to seek out Diverse Delight.

He was certain that she would be well informed about everything.

Accordingly, dressed once again in the plain robe he had worn before, he set off toward the '*House of a Thousand Joys*'.

As Yin had said, the streets were filled with Boxers, whooping, shouting and showing off to the crowds and deeply suspicious of anyone who might be a foreigner or a Christian.

Fortunately Stanton Ware, although tall, was adept at disguise and he remembered one of his teachers saying to him,

"When you do not wish to be noticed, then think yourself invisible. Thoughts are just as important as what you wear. They create an aura, which others can read."

Deliberately, therefore, thinking himself invisible, he passed without incident through the largest crowds and finally reached the Street of Flowers and stopped outside the '*House of a Thousand Joys*'.

He entered and on enquiring for Diverse Delight was taken to her room.

"Are you crazy?" she asked him as soon as they were alone. "How can you walk about Peking now, when, if anyone was suspicious, your life would not be worth a thought?"

"I am safe enough," he replied, "but I need your help. Diverse Delight, because it is hard to find out what is happening."

She looked at him and then she said in a low voice,

"Prince Tuan was here last night."

"What did you learn?"

"He had drunk a great deal and he wished to boast of what he intends to achieve."

"And what is that?" Stanton Ware asked.

Diverse Delight drew nearer to him as she said,

"I did not trust even Happy Hours, with whom he stayed, to repeat everything to me. I listened myself and he is determined that there should be war between your people and ours."

"That is what I expected him to want," Stanton Ware said. "But surely the old Empress cannot be so foolish as to think that China can win with so very few Imperial troops and the ragged and in most cases weaponless Boxers?"

Diverse Delight glanced over her shoulder almost as if she was afraid to speak.

Then she said so softly that Stanton Ware could hardly hear,

"The Prince is most concerned that the looting and terrorism may incense the Dowager Empress against the Boxers."

"That, I should think, is a possibility," Stanton Ware said dryly, thinking of the buildings that he had already seen burning.

"He is therefore concocting a letter," Diverse Delight went on, "supposedly written by the Great Powers, demanding that all the Military forces and all the Chinese revenue should be placed in their hands."

"It is not possible!" he exclaimed. "Would the Empress really believe such nonsense?"

"Prince Tuan is very clever," Diverse Delight replied, "he knows exactly how to sting Her Majesty into action."

Stanton Ware waited, he knew that this was the crux of the whole plot.

"The letter will also demand the restoration of the Emperor's authority," Diverse Delight went on, "and a special residence for him of his own."

Stanton Ware knew that this was real dynamite.

The Dowager Empress had kept her nephew in complete subjection. In fact he had been nothing but a prisoner in the Ocean Palace.

She had further humiliated him by making him attend all the Councils that she presided over, but he was not allowed to speak or express an opinion of any sort.

She was well aware that if the Powers did bolster him up, her ascendancy over him and over the whole country would vanish.

The Chinese had always preferred a man to lead them and in their hearts they had always felt slightly degraded because of the authority assumed by the Dowager Empress.

It was, Stanton Ware thought, a brilliant piece of fantasy on the part of Prince Tuan.

It was useless to say that the Dowager Empress would not believe such a fabrication or have the common sense to realise that the Powers would not attempt in any way to interfere with the governing of China. All they wanted was to trade.

But the Dowager Empress was not a normal, balanced, sensible human being.

She was basically an uneducated but determined amazon of a woman who had risen to power by murder and by every ruthless intrigue it was possible to imagine.

She might dislike foreigners, she might hate their having such a foothold in her country, but, more than anything else, she would fight to the death for her own supremacy.

She would never, and Stanton Ware was quite certain of this, submit to being subservient to her nephew the Emperor.

"What can we do?" he asked despairingly.

Diverse Delight made a little gesture of helplessness with her hands.

"Prince Tuan will win as he has always intended."

CHAPTER SEVEN

Stanton Ware awoke and realised that he was alone on the *K'ang*.

He looked across the room and saw Zivana standing silhouetted against the sunshine, looking out onto the lotus flowers that were in full bloom beneath her.

It was early in the morning and yet already it was very hot.

One wall of the Lotus Pavilion could be folded back so that the whole room was open to what air there was.

Stanton was thinking how beautiful his wife looked and how much he loved her, when, as if she felt his eyes drawing her, she turned round.

When she saw that he was now awake, she ran across the room to kneel on the end of the *K'ang* looking at him.

Her dark hair fell over her shoulders and he thought that every day since their marriage she had grown more beautiful yet at the same time more spiritual.

And he found himself staring at her in amazement.

"You did not awaken me last night," she said and her voice was reproachful.

"You were fast asleep," he answered, "and you looked so very happy dreaming of me that I had not the heart to disturb you."

"How do you know that I was dreaming of you?"

"Who else?" he asked.

He expected her to smile at him, but she replied wistfully,

"I waited for so long. Were you very late?"

"Very," he replied. "Yin and I had to hide ourselves for a very long time until a party of Boxers moved out of sight and we could carry the food into the cellar by the South gate."

Zivana shivered.

She was always afraid when every night Stanton Ware and Yin left the house in disguise to carry food to the Christians who were hiding in many parts of the City.

Zivana knew that without Stanton Ware's help most of these children and many of the women would have died, because by now it was two months since the Boxers had entered Peking.

As if he read her thoughts, he said,

"You are right, they came in on Prince Tuan's orders on June thirteenth and now it is the thirteenth of August."

*

As he spoke, he thought that they had been for him the most wonderful weeks of his life. He had not thought it possible to be so happy or so wildly and so overwhelmingly in love.

Everything about Zivana thrilled him and, although he was carried away by her beauty, he also found her more intelligent to talk to than any woman he had ever known before.

She had not only thought deeply and read extensively in both Chinese and Russian, she was also nearly knowledgeable as he was in the philosophy of both countries.

It was, he knew, all that was spiritual in her make-up which responded to his awareness of the world behind the world.

He could never have loved a woman without that particular quality and so together they would help each other grow nearer every day to the Divine source of all knowledge.

As he felt almost guilty for being so happy when there was so much suffering all round them, he sighed and said,

"It is eight weeks since the siege of the British Legation began."

As Zivana had often heard this before and knew that to talk about it upset him, she said with a little tremor in her voice,

"Was it very – dangerous for you last night?"

"No worse than usual," Stanton replied. "We merely had to wait a long time and that was extremely boring."

"And I was waiting here for – you."

"I knew that."

"But you did not go straight to the South gate?"

"No," he replied. "I went first to call on Diverse Delight before Yin and I picked up the food."

"Again?"

There was a barely perceptible note of sharpness in Zivana's tone.

Now she was not looking at him but out towards the garden, her small straight nose and soft lips silhouetted against the almond-blossom pink of the curtains.

"Why did you say it like that?" he asked. "You know as well as I do that Diverse Delight is the best-informed woman in all – "

He stopped suddenly and then with an amused note in his voice, he asked,

"You cannot be jealous, my precious one?"

Zivana did not reply and after a moment he said,

"Come here. I will explain to you that there is no reason for jealousy."

Still Zivana did not move and after a moment he put out his hand, saying,

"Come to me, Zivana!"

She made no response and he murmured,

"A Chinese wife is always obedient to her Lord and Master!"

"I am not – Chinese," she said almost fiercely. "I am English – obstinate and resentful!"

Stanton Ware laughed and, before she could prevent him, he moved swiftly and, taking hold of her arm, pulled her down beside him.

Her head fell back against the pillows and he was loosening her robe, pulling it aside to kiss the whiteness of her shoulders, the pink tips of her breasts and the softness of her neck.

Half-seriously she tried to remain stiff and indifferent.

Then, as he ignited the fire in her that was never far away, her arms went round him.

"Now I am Russian!" she whispered. "*Very – very – Russian!*"

"And I am a Dragon," he replied, "and you cannot escape for I hold you, my precious pearl, completely and utterly captive."

His lips then came down on hers, the glory of their love enveloped them and her heart was beating beneath his.

*

Later, very much later, holding Zivana close against him, Stanton said,

"I have good news for you."

She looked up at him, her eyelids still heavy from the passion he had evoked in her, her lips soft and warm from the intenseness of his kisses.

"Good news?" she questioned.

"Yes," he replied, "yesterday the sound of Maxim guns was heard in the distance."

"Maxim guns?"

"The guns which only our troops could be firing."

Zivana gave a little cry of delight.

She clung frantically to Stanton Ware as if there were no words and only the closeness of him could express her feelings.

It was summer and a hot wind had blown the sand down into Peking from the deserts of Mongolia.

For the first time the Dowager Empress could not escape to the cool breezes and pools of her expensive Summer Palace, but was forced just like her poorest subjects to cope with the blazing heat of Peking.

In Tseng-Wen's house the heat was not as oppressive as it was elsewhere.

In fact every time Stanton returned from one of his expeditions of mercy he felt the cool moisture in the air was like a long drink to a thirsty man.

This was due, he knew, to the unceasing attentions of the new servants whom Yin had brought into the household.

They spent their time spraying the courtyards, watering the flowers and making all the fountains in the garden rise high towards the sky.

In the deserted gardens of those who had fled the City there were only withered patches of burnt grass and brown petals.

But everything surrounding Zivana was green, moist and fragrant whilst the Pavilion at night was cool and seemed to contain the fragrance of a thousand roses.

The new servants were relatives of Yin who were hiding from the Boxers because one of their sons had attended a Christian school.

The ferocity and brutality of the Boxers towards the Christian converts exceeded even their hatred of the foreigners.

They had taken over the City in a manner that made the Chinese citizens themselves feel that they were a conquered race.

Brandishing ramshackle weapons, they swaggered around the City in their red sashes, burning, killing and creating terror until even Prince Tuan had no control over them.

Banners of gold, scarlet and blue embroidered with emblems, fluttered over the tens of thousands of motley ill-assorted soldiery arrayed outside the terrified Legations.

Every Christian Church had been reduced to smoking ruins with the one exception of the Northern Cathedral, where the Bishop of Peking, with twenty-two Nuns, thirty-four hundred converts and eight hundred children was with unbelievable bravery still withstanding a siege.

It was impossible for Stanton Ware to give them any help but then with the assistance of Yin's relatives and Diverse Delight he managed to keep alive hundreds of other small pockets of refugees.

These consisted of Missionaries, converts and foreigners, who had hidden themselves in all sorts of strange places where the Boxers could not find them.

When his own money had finally run out, he had found to his surprise that Zivana was a great heiress. But it was impossible to draw any money in her name without running the risk of someone being aware that she was in the City.

There was so much conflict going on not only between the Army and the Legations but amongst the Chinese themselves that Stanton knew it was imperative that they should not in any way risk disclosure.

Yin solved the problem by sending out one of his brothers to Tseng-Wen to tell him what was happening.

The moment he returned from the country, all that Stanton required was available.

As Tseng-Wen had many good and trustworthy friends amongst the tradesmen, it was easy for him to buy what rice and grain they required and take it straight from the warehouses to the beleaguered people they assisted.

As he had anticipated, the members of other communities had found the British Legation the safest and the easiest to defend.

If it had not been so dangerous, Stanton Ware would have been amused by the stupidity of Sir Claude Macdonald.

When early in August the first contingent of troops under Admiral Sir Edward Seymour had for a few days been beaten back to the sea, the Dowager Empress, convinced by Prince Tuan's document that all foreigners wished to deprive her of power, had given the Legations twenty-four hours' notice to leave Peking.

When they had heard of the ultimatum, a heated quarrel broke out between the different Ministers.

Sir Claude Macdonald, twirling his waxed moustach, decided that they should obey the Empress, abandon all the Chinese with foreign connections and leave at once.

But Stanton Ware, who had been smuggled into the Legation at night, protested violently as did the Correspondent of *The Times,*

"If you leave Peking tomorrow," they declared to Sir Claude, "the death of every man, woman, and child in this huge and unprotected convoy will be on your head and your name will go down in history and be known as the wickedest, weakest and most pusillanimous coward who ever lived!"

Strong though their arguments were, Sir Claude and the majority of the other Ministers would not listen.

The only one who sided with them and agreed that to surrender the Christian converts in their charge would be unpardonable was the German Minister Baron von Kestler.

He was a florid and excitable man with a flaming temper, who only a few days before had caught a teenaged Boxer outside the Legations and beaten him with a walking stick to within an inch of his life.

He decided to speak to the members of the Dowager Empress's Council personally and set off towards the Forbidden City in his official chair.

On his way there he was shot dead at point-blank range, after which even Sir Claude had to admit that they could no longer leave the City with any hope of safety.

As the last hour of the ultimatum expired, the Chinese Army fired their first volley into the Legation and the siege began.

On June the twenty-fourth the Empress capitulated completely to Prince Tuan's demands and formally acknowledged that the thirty thousand Boxers now in the Capital were Imperial soldiers.

She issued an edict in praise of them, exalting them to 'repel aggression and prove their loyalties without failing to the end'.

She was not so pleased when Prince Tuan, swollen-headed by her compliance with his request, forced his way into the Forbidden City with a number of his Boxers.

He claimed that some of her personal attendants were clandestine Christians and that, if a Boxer struck them on the forehead, a cross would appear.

Immediately he and his followers began striking the screaming eunuchs and the maids.

No crosses appeared, but Diverse Delight then heard that the Dowager Empress was extremely perturbed by the occurrence.

Early on in August the news at last reached Peking that a great force of Allied troops had relieved Tientsin and were on their way to the Imperial City.

Stanton Ware and the Empress learnt that the eighteen-thousand force included Russian, British, American, Japanese and French troops with superior weapons against a Chinese force of twenty-five thousand.

Because it was difficult to obtain reliable news, the British Legation could only continue to fight off their attackers as the women sewed sandbags from monogrammed pillow-cases, silk pyjamas, damask curtains and the best China brocade.

It made the barricades look like a New Year's Carnival, but the Chinese converts did the heavy work and showed, as everyone was to relate later, extreme courage under fire.

It was impossible for Stanton Ware to have any further contact with the Legation, but he was most thankful of one thing, that he had persuaded Herbert Squiers to lay in large stocks of food.

He had learnt that much had been bought by the First Secretary, on his instigation, from the traders he was in contact with.

"Many carts of rice and other food," one of the traders said, "cost big money, but now no one hungry."

It was not entirely true, in fact by the time the siege ended all the Legation's Racehorses and hunters had been killed to provide meat and the Chinese converts had only a sparse diet of grain.

But last night Diverse Delight had told Stanton Ware that the troops were nearing the City and the Dowager Empress was in a frantic state of fear.

"Today," Diverse Delight went on, "she sent for Prince Tuan five times and she ordered the execution of three more Ministers who had advised caution in the Council meetings."

Stanton Ware had looked sad. He well knew that those whom the Dowager Empress had murdered were wise and sensible Statesmen and had only been overruled by the violence of Prince Tuan.

"There is something more I have to tell, which I think will please you," Diverse Delight said.

"What is that?" he asked.

"Today the Empress appointed Li Hung-Chang to be her Plenipotentiary in charge of the peace negotiations."

"That is indeed good news," Stanton agreed.

Li Hung-Chang had left Peking to go to Canton when the Empress refused to listen to his warning.

Although she sent for him again and yet again, he would not return and instead gathered together the Southern Viceroys, who felt just as he did, to suppress not the foreigners but the Boxers.

They agreed that Prince Tuan was an evil influence on the Throne and so did everything they could to defy and nullify his orders.

They refused to send troops to Peking, joined forces with foreign Powers in the Treaty Ports and continued to pay back their loans.

In point of fact Stanton Ware had been so right in saying that only Li Hung-Chang could save China.

It was his courageous unilateral action that saved the country from the full scale war that the Dowager Empress would have brought upon her people.

"There is also bad news," Diverse Delight continued.

"What is that?"

"The old Empress has ordered a Krupp gun to be fitted on the wall of the Imperial City today to bombard the Legations in one last night of siege."

Stanton Ware had stared at Diverse Delight incredulously.

Then, as he wondered what he could do about this information, a warning voice inside him told him that it must be nothing foolish.

His responsibility was towards Zivana and even if he could reach the Legation alive and tell them what they might expect, they could do no more to withstand a further bombardment than they had done already.

"Do those who are besieged know that relief is at hand?" he asked.

When Diverse Delight nodded, his own relief swept some of the anxiety from his eyes.

If the defenders' spirits were riding high, as so they would be, he told himself, the crude reinforcements, the amateur breast-works and the scanty ammunition would hold out until the relief force marched in.

He had left Diverse Delight and gone with Yin to collect grain and then, hearing the explosions from the Krupp gun, he had gone back with a heavy heart.

Yet before he fell asleep beside Zivana he remembered his vision in the Temple and his spirits rose.

He had seen with his own eyes the picture of the troops marching into the City and the walls falling before them.

He had seen too the excitement and rejoicing as the British Legation was relieved and the occupants came rushing out.

How could he doubt for a moment that what he had been permitted to see would be the truth?

Zivana too had looked into the reality of the future. The Dowager Empress, disguised as a peasant woman, would flee from The Palace and with her would go the Emperor and Prince Tuan.

As he awoke, he knew that, if the Legation had fallen during the night, Yin would have awakened him to tell him so.

That he had been allowed to sleep proclaimed that the Krupp gun, just like all the other offensive weapons used by the Boxers and the Imperial troops, had proved ineffective.

"We have all day to ourselves," Zivana said softly, interrupting his thoughts.

"The whole day," he answered. "This is a very strange honeymoon, my precious one, but I would not have it any other way."

"Nor I," she whispered.

"But once Peking is relieved, I intend to take you home."

His voice was calm as he spoke, but his eyes watched her face a little apprehensively as if he thought that she might protest or refuse to contemplate returning to England.

He was ready to tell her that he would have to return in order to make his report to the Prime Minister of what had occurred.

He also wanted his relatives to meet his wife and most of all he longed to see her in the house he owned in the country.

A very fine building, it stood in a large estate of good farming land, which had been the property of the Wares for many generations.

He waited and then Zivana said,

"You know I will go anywhere in the world that you wish me to, but I would above all like to see England, which is not only your land, my darling husband, but that of my mother."

"My precious, you could not have said anything to please me more!" he exclaimed.

He kissed her and added,

"You are so perfect, in what you say, in what you think and in what you do."

His voice was serious as he went on,

"It is not only your beauty, my lovely wife, that holds me completely captive to you now and for all Eternity, but something far more important."

"Tell me," Zivana said caressingly. "You know how I adore to hear you making love to me in words."

"There are other ways I prefer to make love to you," Stanton Ware smiled, "but words, my darling, come to me like poems to extol your virtues and I like to say them aloud because they sound like music."

"You are so wonderful," Zivana said, "so wonderful that I cannot believe you really – belong to me."

"Is that why you were jealous?" he teased her.

"I am jealous in case – Diverse Delight could amuse you as I am – unable to do. I know a great deal about – some things, but very little about – *love*."

"I will teach you all you need to know," Stanton said firmly.

"And suppose you do not – teach me enough and when we return to – England where it is cold I cease to – interest you?"

Stanton Ware laughed and then said,

"England is not half as cold as Peking in the winter and, thank goodness, not so very hot in the summer. But wherever we are, because we are together, because you are you, my love will increase day by day and year by year."

"That is what I want to hear you say," she answered, "and you will love me – even if I am not as – beautiful as you – think me now?"

"To me you will always be the most beautiful woman I have ever seen," Stanton Ware said, "and it will be a long time, my sweet one, before your beauty is full-blown let alone before it begins to fade."

"It is not only age that – changes one's – appearance," Zivana said in a low voice.

Stanton Ware looked puzzled and then he said in a different tone of voice,

"What are you trying to say to me, my precious?"

Zivana made a little movement to hide her face against his shoulder.

He held her very closely.

Then he said,

"I shall begin to guess in a moment."

She raised her eyes to his, they were shining and her lips were smiling.

"I think, darling, that you know why I am – glad to go with you to – England. You would want your – son to be born in your own – house and in your – own land."

Stanton looked down at her.

"You are – sure, my lovely one?"

"As sure as – one can be – so soon," she answered.

"My precious, my darling, my love, my life, my wife!"

Then he was kissing her as if she was not only infinitely precious to him but sacred in a way that she had never been before.

Her arms went round his neck to hold him closer still.

"I love you!" she whispered. "I love you, my fierce, strong gentle Dragon."

"You are mine," he said, and there was wonder as well as a note of possession in his voice. "*Mine*, the Perfect Pearl of love who holds my heart and my soul in her little hands."

Then there was the scent of lilies and the petal softness of her skin against his lips.

Printed in Great Britain
by Amazon